D
C

SUPE

Book 2

THE NEW NORMAL

John Zakour & Katrina Kahler

Table of Contents

Dad...

This was the ending to one of the weirdest times of my life. First I discovered that I have super powers. In fact, all my female ancestors before me had these powers. I am so strong that one of my farts can instantly drop a herd of cows. I can knock people out with a tap or with a whiff of my armpit. My breath can toss people around like a hurricane. I can leap tall buildings. I have a bunch of powers that I don't even understand yet. In other words, I'm super.

Of course, I love to use my powers to help people. I have saved a cute kid from a gorilla in the zoo, a cat from a tree and stopped a bunch of bad guys from robbing people. (Naturally, it's tempting to think about knocking out the mall with super foot odor and having the place to myself. But that's something I would never do.) The press calls me Super Teen and I kind of like that. But as strange as it may be to have super powers, nothing in my life was nearly as strange as seeing my father standing before me.

"Marcus! What are you doing here?" my mom demanded.

"Isabella, you look lovely as ever," he replied.

"Answer the question, Marcus!" Mom was not impressed. I swear I could see steam coming off her body.

Dad held up two hands. "When I saw Super Teen on TV I knew it had to be Lia. I wanted to tell her how proud I am of her. Finally, one of you Strong women is willing to use her powers in the open."

Mom shook her head. "Okay, so why didn't you call and set up a time to come visit?"

"Would you have taken my call?" Dad asked.

"No, probably not," Mom admitted. "But why break into our house in the middle of the night?"

Dad smiled. "I wanted to test Lia's senses and reflexes to see how fast she responded."

"How'd I do?" I asked, more eager than I thought I'd be.

He grinned at me. "Your senses are quite good. I snuck in here very quietly, yet you still reacted in…" he looked at his watch. "Less than 10 seconds." He paused. "Now let's try out your reflexes."
He pushed a button on his watch and a small floating disc hovered into the room.

"Neat drone!" I grinned.

Mom shook her head. "Marcus this is our DAUGHTER, not a test subject!" She put her hands on her hips in protest.

Glancing over at Mom, I saw that her face was creased into a deep frown. She knew where this was heading and didn't seem happy at all.

"Exactly," Dad said. "Just going to have the drone put her through her paces so I can see what she can do." He looked at my mom. "I don't suppose you've trained her?"

"I've given her suggestions and ways to keep her power under control. But I'm a big believer in learning by experience," Mom said slowly, one eye on Dad, the other on the drone.

"Does anyone want to explain to me what's going on here?" I asked.

Dad turned to me. "I'm working for a new company, the one that has the huge facility outside of town. They're called Big Massive Science. I'm head of research which gives me access to all the newest and coolest gadgets." Dad pointed at the floating drone. "This is a self-operating security drone. A few of these babies can protect a building far better than a squad of humans."

Mom crossed her arms. "And what do these have to do with your daughter? The daughter you haven't seen in over a decade," she added.

Dad locked eyes on her. "I took this job with BM Science so I could be closer!"

"And get your hands on the latest gadgets," Mom sighed.

Dad nodded. "Yep, win-win."

The entire time Mom and Dad were talking, the drone hovered above Dad's head. It made a freaky low pitched buzzing sound. I didn't know if regular human ears could hear it, but I certainly could. I heard the sound increase in speed. A red light lit up in the middle of the drone. Something inside of me said, move now. I shot to the left. A beam of energy fired from that red dot, burning a hole in the floor. A hole right where my foot had been just a second earlier.

"What the...?" I shouted.

Dad clapped his hands excitedly. "Excellent move, my daughter!"

"Marcus!" Mom screamed. "This is your daughter you're attacking here!"

Dad shook his head. "Not attacking! Testing. If I were attacking I would have brought more than one. Besides I'm sure she can handle it!"

Yeah, now I could see why Mom didn't last all that long with Dad. He had kind of complete tunnel vision.

"Honey, do you want me to take this thing out?" Mom asked, looking at me.

I locked my eyes on the drone. I hated to admit it, but I wanted my dad to be pleased with me. "I've got this!" I said confidently.

Dad clapped again. "I've never been prouder of my own flesh and blood."

"You'd better hope you don't see any of her blood," Mom said, fist shaking at Dad.

I was pretty sure he didn't hear her as his concentration was locked on the drone and me. It hovered closer to me. Still out of my reach, but closer. I swatted at it just to see how it would react. It darted back and then fired a beam of energy at my midsection. I jumped over the beam. It left a burn mark on the wall.

"I'll have the company pay for any damages!" Dad said, ignoring Mom's shocked reaction at the sight of her living room being destroyed.

The drone began dropping and then rising very quickly. It fired at me again. I saw the blast and leaned to the side but the beam still hit me in the arm, burning through my robe.

"Hey! This is my favorite robe!" I shouted at the drone. I lunged towards it. It darted to the side. I fell on my face. I swear the drone laughed at me. It then dived for my behind, hitting me with another laser sting.

"Ouch!" I screamed jumping to my feet and rubbing my butt at the same time. I spun at the drone, trying to bat it down with my hands. It darted away, and at the same time fired another bolt of energy at me. This one hitting me in the knee. It stung!

I lunged at the drone again. It dodged me once more. But this time as I fell to the ground, I forced out a fart. Not a silent one either. This fart made the room shake. The power from my fart shattered the drone into millions of tiny drone pieces. I smiled as I watched the pieces crumble to the ground. I heard another clunk. My dad laid there on the floor, stiff as a board.

Mom ran up to me and put her arm around me. "Great use of pressure and gas!" she said.

I looked over at dad. "I feel bad about him though!"

Mom shook her head. "Don't! He brought this upon himself. I don't know what I ever saw in the man." She knelt down beside him to take his pulse. "He didn't take a direct hit, so he should be fine."

She grabbed a vase from a table. The flowers in it had wilted. Mom showed me the wilted flowers.

"This is why we can't have nice things," she kidded.

She then tossed the water from the vase into my dad's face. He shivered, his eyes popping open. "Wow, what amazing power!" he said, gazing at the shattered drone. "More amazing…that thing is bullet proof!" He sat up and took hold of my arm that the drone had shot. He looked at it carefully. "Fascinating! You don't have a burn mark or even a scratch!"

Mom pulled Dad up to his feet. "Yeah, but you didn't know she was that durable when you brought your attack drone here!" she complained angrily, putting a fist under his chin.

Grabbing Mom's arm, I pulled it away from Dad's face. "Mom, he's a scientist like you, he had to test me!" I tried to convince her, but it wasn't working.

She shook her head. "I heal people. I don't hurt them." She leaned into my dad and growled, "Not unless they attack my baby girl!"

Dad lifted his hands up again. "Not an attack, just a test. And she's no baby. She's grown into quite the woman. Smart and powerful!"

"First thing you said that I agree with," Mom told him. "Next time you want to see our daughter, I expect a phone call. I also expect you to come without test droids or robots or clones or anything else that might harm her. She's your DAUGHTER, not a test subject!"

Dad nodded in agreement. "I have a small living quarters in the basement of the lab. If you need me, you can find me there." He looked again at the dust that was the drone. "Man, they are going to dock my pay for this."

Mom lifted him off the ground. "You didn't tell anybody else about Lia? Did you?"

Dad smiled at her. "No, of course not. I'm fully aware that many of my colleagues wouldn't understand her like I do. I also understand the need for secrecy and privacy. I'm here solely as a father and a scientist."

Mom dropped him to the ground. "Fine."

He turned towards the window but Mom grabbed him firmly by the shoulder, stopping him in his tracks. "If you ever come again unannounced, I will have you arrested."

Dad nodded. "Understood."

He started to climb out the window. He then paused for a moment and looked back at me. "Nice seeing you again, honey. It's amazing what you've become." He blew me a kiss. That felt better than I thought it would.

I watched him drop out the window. Yep, I have a really bizarre life now, I thought.

Mom shook her head and repeated once more. "I don't know what I ever saw in that man!"

"I do!" I told her. "He's smart and dedicated just like you!" I gave her a hug.

"Yeah, I guess he does have some good points!" she agreed, hugging me back tightly. "Plus, he is kind of cute with that brown hair and green eyes." Sighing, she shook her head. "Of course if he ever comes here unannounced again, I'll squish him like a bug!"

She broke away from our hug then put an arm around me and started leading me towards the stairs. "We need to get some sleep, both of us have a busy day tomorrow."

"Yep, I don't believe life is ever going to return to normal," Sighing loudly, I climbed the stairs alongside her.

She grinned at me. "Of course it will, it will be a new normal. From now on, super is your normal. Yes, it is a lot of responsibility but I'm sure you can handle it. You're far more mature at your age than I was."

She kissed me on the forehead and I went to my room.

But I laid awake for a while in bed. I'd seen my dad for the first time in years! Sure, he broke into our house and brought a security drone to test me. Yeah, he had me attacked and yes, those energy blasts did sting. And yep, he seemed more interested in what I could do than who I was. But I still felt good that I had finally seen him again and that he wanted to be a part of my life. Plus, he blew me a kiss and said he was proud of me and was even impressed by me. Seriously, the man took a job here just to be near me and Mom. That takes some guts, especially knowing that if he made Mom mad, she'd pretty much pound him down.

I dozed off thinking how nice it was to have my father back in my life. Sure these weren't the most ideal situations. But things in life are hardly ever perfect. I mean look at me. I'm way strong and have all these cool powers, which is neat; yet one slip-up, one mistimed fart, and everybody around me is out cold on the ground; my reputation ruined forever. I felt pretty certain that a whiff of my feet on a hot day could drop a squad of navy seals, the toughest Navy men alive – even if they had gas masks on. So yeah, life was not perfect. But you take the cool with the not so cool. There is always a tradeoff, that's just how the universe works.

I was super!! I had a mom who loved me. I had a Grandma and a Great Grandma who loved me. I had awesome friends! And now my dad was back in my life. I'll take it!

Dear Diary: This is my very first official written entry as a super teen. And…Wow! Wow! Wow! Not only am I super, but I have my dad back in my life. Not sure what is cooler. I guess the super powers. But it is nice having my dad around, even if it might be just to study me. Regardless of his flaws, he is a dedicated scientist and much like Mom. Sure Mom heals people, but Dad's inventions could help the entire world. So he is trying to better the world in his own way. He's just like Mom and I. That's what Mom loved about him in the first place. At least, that's my guess.

I could be wrong, after all, I'm just a teen. I haven't even had a real relationship yet. Not a boyfriend – girlfriend type of relationship. Although I do enjoy the way Jason and I get along, even though we're just friends. At least for now, maybe forever. Maybe not. I guess time will tell.

Schooling...

I'm happy (and a little shocked) that the rest of the school week went fairly smoothly. Mr. P, our history teacher assigned us a report, on our family history. In a way, that could be kind of fun. I had the neat advantage of having my grandma and my great grandma around to talk to. The bad thing was that it had to be an oral presentation. I would need to talk for 10 minutes in front of the class. My heart pounded and raced just thinking about it. But I could deal with that, it was a normal kid problem.

Of course, it wouldn't be my life if a few unique events didn't happen. One of them involved a new girl in school. Mr. Ohm told us her name was Jessie when he introduced her in homeroom. She was tall with long wavy reddish brown hair and creamy white skin.

Krista saw her and said, "Wow! She could be a model, and probably a dancer as well."

The new girl definitely had a cool vibe going on and we were sure she'd fit straight in with the cool group in our grade. But our mouths fell open (especially Jason's and Tim's) when at lunch she passed on sitting at the cool kids' table and chose ours instead.

"Can I sit with you guys?" she asked with a friendly smile.

"Sure!" I said.

"Of course!" Krista added.

Jason and Tim just nodded, their mouths wide open and still in shock. Not a good look on them.

Jessie sat down and began to eat.

"We thought you'd want to sit with them," Krista indicated to the group sitting behind us.

"Ah, no," Jessie replied.

"Why is that?" Krista prodded.

"They don't look like a group I'd fit into," Jessie replied, nibbling on a carrot. She pulled a book out of her bag and began to read it.

"Where you from?" I asked.

"Sun City," she said, looking at me before turning back to her book.

"Ah, what do you like to do?" Krista coaxed.

"Dancing and reading," Jessie added. "Now if you don't mind, I'd really like to get back to this book. I'm right in the middle of a really good part." She turned all her attention to the book she had open in front of her.

That's how our meeting with Jessie continued. She sat and read while Krista and I talked, and Jason and Tim stared at her.

When Jessie finished her food she stood up and said, "Thanks for letting me sit with you. It was nice chatting." Picking up her tray, she walked away.

"Wow!" Krista and I both said in disbelief.

"Wow!" Jason and Tim said in awe.

Krista turned to the guys. "She hardly said a thing!"

"Sure she did!" Tim said, coming out of his Jess inspired daze. "She answered all your questions!"

"But she didn't offer any conversation of her own!" I glanced at him with a shake of my head.

Jason shrugged. "She's probably shy." He sighed, "Wow! Good looking and shy. What a combo!"

"But, but..." Krista stammered.

Patting Krista on the back I told her, "Let it go, girl. These guys aren't thinking straight right now."

"I admit she is really pretty!" Krista commented.

"Sure is!" Jason agreed.

"Understatement of the year!" Tim added.

"Besides, you guys get the same way whenever Brandon comes around!" Jason insisted. He finished his statement by batting his eyes and pretending to faint.

"That's so true!" Tim said, nodding his head firmly.

"But that's different!" Krista said.

"How?" Jason asked.

"Yeah how?" Tim mimicked.

Krista looked at me pleadingly for help.

I shrugged. "Sorry, girlfriend you are on your own here," I told her.

"Okay, it's not different," Krista sighed.

"So the boys' lacrosse team is playing well," I said, keen to change the subject.

"Not as well as the girls' team," Tim answered. "Man, you girls have been lighting it up in practice!"

Krista nodded. "Yes, my girl, Lia has been extra hot."

Jason just smiled at me.

Speaking of lacrosse, it seemed to be progressing well for my new normal. Sure, Wendi gave me hard times about it and said that I needed to lose a pound or two. She also said my wrist shot needed work. But even so, it was nothing I couldn't handle. Every once in a while Lori would put her stick in my face to try to get into my head. I was half tempted to run by her and drop her with a silent fart. But that wouldn't be right. Plus, I didn't have too much control of that particular power. I'd probably drop the whole team. So I decided that would not be cool. Instead, I dealt with it like any normal girl. I pretty much ignored it.

After each practice, Coach Blue would come over to me and let me know I was playing very well. She wanted to put me on the first line with Wendi. I could feel Wendi's eyes beating into me whenever the coach talked to me. I let the coach know that for now, I'd be more comfortable staying on the second line. I told her my knee was sore and thought extra playing time would make it worse.

Truthfully, not only did I not want to play on Wendi's line, I wasn't sure if using my powers was cheating. Technically I guess it wasn't, it was just me being me. I also worked really hard not to use my powers during practice or games. The problem was, it was an unfair advantage over the others and I still didn't know how to deal with that. But I figured I'd figure it out.

I walked home with Jason after practice, and we chatted the way we usually do. The talk started off all normal. Like how Jason didn't love lacrosse but he enjoyed the running and the friendships he'd made on the team. Plus, with him playing on the team, it allowed us to continue the tradition we'd had since grade school of walking home together. I talked about how I still needed to find a way to balance my powers with my playing. While I had to admit I loved showing up Wendi and rushing through Lori, I didn't want to win games that way. I just didn't know how to go about it all. Jason said he had faith in me. He knew I'd figure out the proper course of action. Yes, those were the exact words he used. He could be such a geek sometimes.

Which brought us to this weird conversation we had.

"So, I've been thinking about ways for you to maximize the use of your powers!" Jason told me.

"Okay, I'm always open to ideas."

He hesitated, walking slower. "I thought you could use another long distance weapon. Something more controllable and less devastating than your farts or foot sweat."

"I'm a lady," I said pretending to act all dignified. "I don't fart, I have wind. I don't sweat, I glow."

"Yeah, well, your wind and glow can drop an army," Jason said.

"Sadly, that's true," I laughed.

"You told me that when your dad made a drone attack you, you destroyed it with a fa- I mean wind…"

"Yeah, I did."

"But your wind also clobbered your dad and killed all the plants?"

"What are you getting at, Jason?"

He stopped walking, his eyes open wide. "What if instead of farting, you pulled a booger from your nose and flicked it at the drone?"

"Oh gross!" I said sticking my tongue out. "Girls don't have boogers!"

"I think it would work and be way less lethal," Jason insisted.

I stopped walking. All of a sudden, I understood exactly what he was attempting to do. It made perfect sense in a really gross way. But I was still unsure because it was so disgusting.

"I'm not sure I like the image of me picking my nose and firing what I find at a target," I told him. "Not lady like at all. Plus, if you really must know, I don't have any boogers!" I insisted.

Jason rubbed his chin. "Hmm, that could be true. You might process air and dust differently to regular people."

"Yeah, I guess," I said.

"Toe jam?" Jason asked.

I stuck my tongue out. "If I did have toe jam I'd have to take my shoes off to collect it, which would defeat the entire purpose of finding a long range weapon for me that wouldn't clobber everything around me. Plus my toe jam might end up being a weapon of mass destruction!"

Jason nodded. "Very good point." He rubbed his head. His eyes flashed wide open. "Your spit!"

"Excuse me!"

Jason rubbed his hands together. "Your spit. You could use that as a controlled weapon."

I shook my head. "Girls don't spit!"

He held up a finger. "But they could, they just don't. And I bet your spit could take down a fighter jet. If you needed it to."

I considered what Jason had said. It made sense in a weird sort of gross way. It would be handy to have some sort of long range stealth attack that I could control. One that wasn't potentially lethal to everybody around me.

"Okay, say I wanted to test this super spit out. How could I do it without hurting anybody or destroying anything useful?" I asked.

Jason smirked. I could tell he'd been thinking about this. "The old abandoned quarry. Lots of rocks you could blow up with nobody around. We could go home, get our bikes and ride there in like 10 minutes." He was shaking with excitement.

For a brief moment, I considered jumping us there. But then I figured that might be noticed by some people. Plus I had never jumped while holding another person. That might really hurt Jason. Instead, I nodded in agreement and we raced home to get our bikes.

When we reached the quarry, we found that a large metal fence with sharp edges on the top surrounded it.

Jason looked at the fence and commented, "It's obvious they don't want anybody in there. But you could jump over that fence easily. I won't be able to get over it though." His eyes popped open again. "Unless you carried me over it?"

"It might not be safe," I warned.

He waved a hand at me. "I trust you."

Okay, this would take a little planning on the best way to jump a metal fence while carrying another person. Apparently, though, Jason had been thinking about this since learning about my powers.

"You can just give me a piggy back jump!" he told me.

I turned and let him grab onto my back. He lifted his legs up and I grabbed hold of them, then gave him a piggy back ride to the fence. Once there, I bent down. "Are you sure about this?" I asked over my shoulder.

"Yeppers!" he said.

I leaped upwards and forward. We easily cleared the fence. I landed face first in the dirt. Jason bounced off me the second my face made contact with the ground. He went rolling forward maybe ten feet, maybe more. I pushed myself up, spat dirt out of my mouth and rushed over to him. He was on the ground face first. He got to his feet, laughing. Breathing a sigh of relief, I watched as my sigh knocked him back down.

"Sorry," I grinned, extending him my hand.

He took it, and I pulled him to a standing position. After dusting himself off, he grinned back. "That's the price I have to pay for having a super best friend!"

We headed over to the quarry, a big massive hole of hard rock. Standing on the edge and looking down, all we could see was brown rock. Across the pit were a few big boulders lining the edge of the crater.

Jason pointed at one of them. "Okay, that's your target!"

I had to admit, collecting a bunch of spit in my mouth felt weird. I rolled my tongue around my cheek until I thought I had a decent amount of spit collected. I puffed my lips and blew the spit out. It went flying across the quarry but didn't come close to where I had aimed. Instead, it hit a spot much lower on the opposite side. But the force left a large hole in the wall. Debris from that hole crumbled down deeper into the quarry.

"Wow!" Jason said leaping up and down. "That's got more fire power than a cannon!"

"Yeah, but my aim is terrible," I complained.

He patted me on the shoulder. "We'll work on that!"

I spent the next thirty minutes or so practicing aiming my spit. Now, that's something I never thought I'd say. Jason worked with me to get my super eye sight to lock on the target. Finally, after I don't know how many shots and even more destruction, I hit the boulder I had aimed at. My spit shattered the boulder into dust.

Jason patted me on the back. "I knew you could do it!"

"Glad one of us did," I laughed.

Jason and I stayed at the quarry practicing until we both got hungry. When my rumbling stomach began to shake the walls of the quarry, we headed back home. But instead of leaping the fence this time, I used my hands to break it apart. Once Jason had walked through, I tied it back together.

When I finally arrived home, Mom asked me where I'd been.

"Destroying rocks with my spit," I explained.

She laughed.

Yeah, my new normal was certainly not all that

normal.

Dear Diary: I'm not sure what to make of this Jessie girl. She's so perfect looking, yet strange acting. Yeah, she might just be shy but a strange feeling in my gut tells me there's something else going on with her. The way Jason and Tim (and the other boys and some of the girls) look at her doesn't seem natural. Maybe I'm being silly, but just because I'm super, doesn't mean I can't be jealous.

When I checked out what was being posted on my social media pages, I saw that everybody in the school was talking about Jessie. The amazing thing seemed to be that she didn't seem to have Facebook, Instagram, Twitter or Snapchat. Well, there were no accounts that anyone could find. Wendi thought that was weird. Wendi also couldn't believe that Jessie would choose not to sit at her table.

In the end, Wendi decided that Jessie had to be a freak, a sort of pretty freak. For once I kind of agreed with Wendi (though not publicly....) Jessie was different. But that's really something coming from ME. The girl whose spit can knock holes in the sides of mountains. Surely, there could be no one as different as that!

Elephant on the run....

Ah, how l love my Saturday mornings. I just get to lay in bed and sleep and take it easy. It so good to relax after a long school week. This week had not only seemed extra-long but it was mega crazy. Lying in bed gave me a chance to recharge.

My phone started vibrating and beeping from the night stand next to my bed.

I knew that beep to mean an incoming social media post. Then I got another and another and another. Yeah, that was way too much action for so early on a Saturday morning. Most of my friends should still be sleeping right then. Even Jason liked to sleep until at least 9 on Saturdays.

Another beep. This was a different sound and I knew it meant a text from Jason. I picked up my phone. It was 9:15.

JASON> Turn on TV – Channel 13…Zoo again!

I grabbed the remote, which I also kept on my night stand. Clicking the TV, I scrolled impatiently through the channels to number 13, looking for the local news segment. When I finally found it, I saw a man in a suit reporting into the camera, "This is Oscar Oranga for Channel 13, Live Witness News. We bring you the news faster and better than the others! We are reporting from the zoo for the second time in a week! This time one of the elephants, a 10-year-old male named Bumbo, has broken free of its home. Bumbo is now running amok in the zoo! We can only hope Super Teen is awake and watching!"

Well, Super Teen wasn't quite awake but she was certainly watching. Surely the zoo staff could handle this? Another text popped onto my phone.

JASON>You're going to help, right?

LIA>OMW

I hopped out of bed, picking up a shirt laying on the floor beside my laundry basket. It was one I'd worn recently at the gym so I sniffed the under arm area just to be sure. OMG! That had some kick to it. I needed a different outfit with more style and less odor. I pulled out a cute pink top with long sleeves and the face of a teddy bear stitched onto the front. It was one I'd never worn but thought it would be a great disguise. At least it was something that no one had ever seen me wear before. Then I grabbed a pair of green skinny jeans covered in a cool star pattern. They were new ones that Mom had recently bought for me. I pulled the tags off and threaded a pink studded belt through the loops to complete the outfit. Taking a quick check in the mirror, I grinned, pleased with the result. It actually looked quite good. If I was going to be in the media, at least I could look reasonably decent. Grabbing my mask, I pushed it firmly onto my head and pulled up the window. Within seconds, I was roof hopping to the zoo.

Having done this before, helped to make my journey to the zoo grounds fairly quick. I was kind of proud of how smoothly it all went. As I headed in the direction that people were fleeing from, I saw that the elephant had left a long trail of destruction.

I didn't need my super vision to spot the large animal running down the zoo concourse. The poor thing seemed scared. I knew it didn't want to hurt anybody and I certainly didn't want to hurt it. I ran towards it, not quite sure how I would handle the issue, but figured I'd work it out when I got there.

However, standing right in front of the charging elephant, I spotted a very familiar little blond boy, my neighbor, Felipe.

"Calm down, Bumbo, calm down!" Felipe coaxed, trying to stay calm himself.

Of course, the Channel 13 film crew stood there filming and not doing much else.

I leaped between Felipe and Bumbo.

Facing Felipe, I told him, "Don't worry, everything is going to be okay!"

Not even a second later, I was run over by the elephant. He must have hit me with his head and then trampled over me with his legs. The only thing it hurt though, was my ego. Yeah, not a bright move turning my back on a charging elephant.

Pushing up off the ground, I leaped onto Bumbo's back. I knew that trying to reason with a frightened charging elephant wouldn't work. No use even trying. Instead, I tightened my legs around Bumbo's back and squeezed. I certainly didn't want to hurt the big guy but I really had to put him down before he ran over Felipe.

The elephant staggered forward a few more steps. By his hesitant movements I could tell that he felt some pain. I squeezed my legs a little harder. I didn't want to kill him, but I knew he must be stopped. Weird, how I had to worry about being so strong I could accidentally squish an elephant.

The second squeeze worked. Bumbo crumbled to the ground. Listening with super hearing, I picked up the sound of his heart still beating. Breathing a sigh of relief, I realized I'd just squeezed the wind out of him. Pulling my leg out from underneath, I stood up, my clothes covered with dirt. I could only guess that my hair looked a mess as well. So, of course, that was when Oscar Oranga stuck a microphone in my face.

"Super Teen! Do you have anything to say about saving the day?" he asked with far more excitement in his voice than was normal.

"Just helping," I said, trying to sound as grown up and adult like as possible.

Felipe ran over and hugged me.

"Wow, this is golden for the camera!" Oscar said, almost giddy with delight.

"Thanks for saving me again!" Felipe said.

"You certainly spend a lot of time at the zoo!" I told him.

"My dad is a veterinarian here!" Felipe announced proudly. "He works with the big cats." Taking a step back from me, he smiled, his eyes alight with excitement.

Felipe's dad ran up to him and hugged him. "Son, that was brave of you to try to calm Bumbo, but you could have been badly hurt!"

"Don't worry, Dad. I knew Super Teen would come and save us both!" Felipe replied with a grin.

Another zoo doctor appeared and placed a stethoscope on Bumbo to check him out.

"Thank you," Felipe's dad turned to me, gratefully. "I'm so glad you arrived in time!"

The other vet looked up, smiled and gave us a thumb

up. "Bumbo is fine. Strangely enough, he seems to be sleeping."

The huge crowd of onlookers began to clap.

"Do you want me to put him back where he belongs?" I asked.

"If you could manage it that would be great!" Felipe's dad replied.

I gently picked Bumbo up and hoisted him over my shoulder. Then I walked him back to the elephant area like a regular person would carry a loaf of bread. As I walked, the doctors and the camera crew followed my every step. I felt good and weird at the same time. Reaching the elephant area, I laid Bumbo down gently on a grassy spot near the water and patted him. When I felt assured he was okay, I leaped up into the air and bounded away!

Dear Diary: OMG! That was soo fun!! I love using my strength to help people like that. It's such a good feeling! Plus it's so great to know I can knock out an elephant by just loosely tightening my legs around its belly. I mean it was crazy. I actually had to concentrate and be careful when dealing with a fully-grown massive elephant so I wouldn't cause any serious injuries. I also have to admit it was pretty cool to be able to carry an elephant on my shoulder like a peanut. All the while, the TV cameras filmed it for the world and my friends to see. That sure felt good getting some nice positive press. Woot!

When I checked my social media pages, I found they were blowing up with people saying how amazing Super Teen was. A few, actually more than a few, commented on how much they liked my outfit. I think that felt as good as being known for carrying around an elephant. Of course, Wendi insisted that Super Teen had to be some sort of trick or publicity stunt for a TV show or something. No matter what, Wendi said she knew for a fact, Super Teen wasn't that super. One thing that was always consistent in my life was Wendi being Wendi.

Oh, side note, the way Felipe looked at me after I saved

him…I got the feeling that he knew who I was. But nah, no way a seven-year-old boy could figure that out. None of the media or my class mates had come close. Even Krista and Tim were wondering yesterday who the heck this mystery girl was. Could she go to our school? Was she home schooled? Haha! I guess Felipe just looked at everybody like he knew them. He was just a friendly outspoken little kid. Nothing wrong with that.

I was also relieved to find Mom understood me going to the zoo and saving the day. She understood that I wanted to help make the world a better place with my powers. She told me she was worried (cause she is a mom) but proud of me. My grandma and my great grandma also sent me texts, telling me how cool it was.

So awesome!

Dinner...

For dinner, Mom and I headed to my favorite hibachi restaurant: A Taste of Japan. Okay, not the best name, but the food there is excellent. I just love hibachi. There's something about watching a guy with sharp knives cut and toss around your food in front of you while he cooks it that just makes the food feel fresher. Kind of makes me feel like one with the meal. I also loved sushi appetizers. Nothing better than the way raw fish feels in the mouth, kind of a nice gooey squish. Of course, Mom and I were careful to be careful with the garlic and onions. Mom joked about the fact that neither of us had dates, so we could indulge a little. She ate a few more than me since she had perfected the art of not gassing the room.

I felt like a nice regular girl again. Yeah, being super is cool but it's great to do normal things as well.

"What on earth is this!" we heard a man yell way louder than was necessary.

Turning towards the sound, I saw a huge man at the bar. He pounded on the counter and scolded the waitress, Lee Tang, "This stuff is raw!"

"Sir, you ordered eel...." Lee said, stepping back.

I know Lee, she's a big sister to Mia, who's in my class. They're both nice quiet girls. They are friendly and smart. Mia was also in the restaurant cleaning tables with a big towel.

The man pounded his fist on the sushi bar again.

"Yeah, but I thought you'd toss it on the fire!" He shook his fist and his face had turned bright red with anger.

This got the chef to come to Lee's aid.

"Sir, sushi is uncooked, raw!" the chef explained.

"I don't even eat my veggies raw!" the man spat. "I'm

not a bird!"

"Sir, birds don't eat a lot of veggies," Lee said poking her head out from behind the chef.

The man crossed his arms. "I'm not paying!!" He pounded the bar again.

Now all eyes in the restaurant were on the man.

Mom groaned. "I know that man. He's George Banks a guy from my class when I was at school, he's always been a jerk."

"We have to do something about him!" I said.

Mom shook her head. "We have to pick out battles. Lee's dad can handle him."

I knew mom had a good point. I felt a little embarrassed that I hadn't figured out the chef was Lee's dad. Still, I didn't appreciate this man being so rude. I glared at him. A beam of energy shot from my eyes and hit the man in the butt. His pants burst into flame!

George stood there frantically trying to blow the fire on his butt out.

"Oops! Looks like you have heat ray vision when you're angry," Mom whispered to me.

Yep, I had just figured that out.

The smoke detectors started beeping. Mom leaped up and raced over to George. "Drop and roll, George. Drop and roll…."

He looked at her. "Wait! Aren't you Isabelle Strong from my class at school?"

"Now it's Doctor Isabelle Strong… drop and roll…" Mom pointed to the ground and spun her finger around.

George dropped to the ground and started rolling as instructed. Mom took a towel from Mia and dropped it over George's big backside. "Call 911!" Mom ordered. She turned to George and patted him gently on the shoulder. "You're going to be alright…. You won't be able to sit on your behind for a day or two but you will live."

"It hurts," George groaned. "Their fire made me catch

on fire...I'll sue..."

"There's no fire going on in the restaurant right now, George," Mom told him. She showed him a burnt lighter. "I removed this from your pocket before I covered you. Looks like your back pocket caught on fire because of the lighter."

"Oh..." George looked at it in confusion.

"Another reason to not smoke," Mom added, just as the paramedics arrived.

"Wait, your name is still Strong? Did you never get married?"

"Got married but kept the name."

"Bummer! I was hoping I'd have a shot with you."

"The EMTs are here to take you to the ER. Don't worry, just first degree burns. You'll be fine."

"Hopefully there won't be any brain damage," Mom mumbled as they took George away.

"Why didn't you tell him you were divorced?" I kidded.

"Quiet and eat your food," she scolded with a smile.

"Heat ray vision is so cool," I said. "Well actually hot, but a cool power to have!"

Mom nodded. "We're going to have to work on training you to stay calm. Don't want you drilling holes in people or melting them when you get angry."

I nodded. "That's a good idea! Otherwise, some of my teachers and also Wendi could soon become dust!"

Dear Diary: Wow, I can fire flames of fire from my eyes. Actually, Mom says it's not technically fire, it's a beam of intense heat that can cause anything it comes in contact with to burn. My mom is such a science geek. But I get it. It's a cool but dangerous weapon that I have to be careful with. It may not have the mass effect of a super fart or super foot odor but it can still be quite hazardous.

Part of me loves the idea of having heat vision. I don't need the microwave to warm up my food or do popcorn. Well, with practice I won't. But another part of me realizes I have to stay calm so this doesn't just blast out of me.

As we walked home, Mom and I worked on my breathing and meditation exercises to quieten my mind and anger as Mom put it. Whenever I feel angry or upset I need to close my eyes, take deep breaths and let them out. I need to count backward from 10 and keep breathing until I feel calm again. Of course, I also have to be careful not to clobber things with my breath.

Being super can definitely be super tricky!

Sunday Trip to the Mall...

Sunday was usually the day I hung out with Tim, Jason, and Krista. Today though, instead of just hanging out with the guys, playing video games and tossing LAX balls around, Krista asked me if I would go to the mall with her to help choose some new shoes.

As it was such a beautiful day, Krista and I decided to walk. Jason told me to take my mask and a change of clothes just in case, so I did. Luckily my new Super Teen outfit had been washed since my episode at the zoo. I wasn't sure why Jason thought Super Teen would be needed at the mall, but I trusted his gut feelings.

"So have you started your genealogy report for history yet?" Krista asked me as we walked.

I shook my head. "Mom wanted me to talk with my grandma and my great grandma today but the weather is so great. I just couldn't do it. Maybe later."

"Your grandmas look so young still! They look like they could be sisters!" Krista said. "Have they had any work done on their skin?"

I shook my head. "Nope, just good genes," I said. I didn't tell her she'd be shocked if she met my great, great grandma who poses as my great grandma's sister now. Yep, whatever makes us super causes us to age really slowly. The good news is we are young for a long time. The sad news is every Strong woman has outlived their husbands by a good deal. Like Grandma would always tell me, life has tradeoffs. But I tried not to think of that as Krista and I entered the mall. I certainly didn't want to focus on the negatives.

We headed right to our favorite store: Shoes! Shoes! Shoes!

Okay, the name wasn't original but the shoes were reasonably priced and so nice. I was wearing some black canvas sneakers and had sprayed my feet really well with Mom's super deodorant. I was certain I could take my shoes off without worrying about knocking out the store. We were there for Krista's shopping spree but I wanted to be prepared just in case.

Before reaching the store, we noticed a crowd gathered in the concourse. There in the middle of the crowd, stood a tall man in a lab coat. He stood next to what I could only describe as a white, life-like, crash-test dummy. The man in the lab coat pointed at the crash-test dummy.

"This, my friends, is BM Science's prototype home health aide robot, HAR!" the man said. The man turned to the robot. "HAR, take a bow."

HAR bowed. "So glad to meet you all!" he or it said.

"HAR is very strong!" the man said.

HAR walked over and picked the scientist up in his arms. The crowd clapped. "We believe HAR is the future of home health aide. He can handle almost any situation."

Krista nudge me. "This is cool. But I want shoes."

I grinned. "Let's head to the store."

In Shoes! Shoes! Shoes! Krista and I could barely contain ourselves. She tried on a really cool pair of red converse high tops and then decided to try some other colors. We both looked at the heels but knew there was no way our moms would approve. Just as I picked up another pair of shoes, I heard a scream, "Help! This thing is crazy!"

The manager of the store ran out towards the scream, but a split second later came rolling back into the store. Right behind him was HAR, the not so helpful robot.

"I'm going to clean you up!" HAR shouted.

The scientist guy ran behind HAR desperately trying to slow him down. "HAR! Stop! Stop!" He demanded. HAR ignored the scientist and picked up the manager with one arm.

HAR turned to the scientist. "I'm cleaning them because dirt causes disease!"

"But why are you hurting people?" the scientist yelled.

HAR locked his head on him. "Must destroy anything that is dirty!" he insisted.

I tugged on Krista. "Let's get out of here," I coaxed.

Krista shook her head. "Nah, I want to see how this plays out!"

I slipped out of the store, telling Krista I had to go to the bathroom. Moving at super speed, I headed quickly off and looked for the nearest facility. Jumping into a stall, I put on my change of clothes and my mask. Then I tossed the clothes I'd been wearing into my canvas carry bag and stashed it up high out of sight.

Rushing back towards the shoe store, my heart started to race. I felt it pounding in my chest. I had sweat forming on my forehead. My palms were clammy. I had no idea how strong this freaky bot was. But I knew I had to stop it.

When I ran back into the store, I saw the HAR holding the store manager and his scientist handler up in the air. He held them over his head like they weighed nothing.

"Hey, why not pick on somebody your own strength?" I asked in my most mocking voice.

HAR spun his head around to look at me without moving his body. It gave me the shivers. He dropped the two men to the ground. HAR turned towards me and started rubbing his hands together anxiously.

"Finally, I get to clean up the mess that is Super Teen!" he shouted. He pointed at me with a plastic white finger. "That pink t-shirt you're wearing doesn't go well with green skinny jeans and white shoes! Where's your sense of color?"

I stomped towards him. "I'm not dressed for a fashion parade!" I told HAR. "But this outfit is still pretty cool!"

HAR bent over and laughed while pointing at me. "Ha! Simple human... You're so funny!"

"You going to stop this craziness?" I asked.

HAR bent his robotic knee joints and raised his fists in front of his plastic face. "Hardly."

"You're an aide robot, not a fighter!" I said.

"I know how to adapt!" He shouted, lunging forward and punching me in the nose.

I gave him credit. I felt that punch, but my head didn't flinch at all. HAR pulled back his fist and looked at it, taking in the dented metal that was the size and shape of my nose.

"Nice try!" I said. I reached up and grabbed HAR by

the top of his head. I pushed down hard. HAR's body buckled under the pressure like a collapsing spring. Maintaining the same level of force, I acted like a human trash compactor reducing HAR to the size of a lunch box. He'd be no more trouble now.

The people in the store began to applaud!

The store manager ran up to me. "That was amazing!" he said, as he breathed a huge sigh of relief.

"It was nothing!" I replied. Although I'd actually been super nervous, it had turned out to be very easy.

"That crazy mad robot was right about something though!" The manager said and pointed at my feet. "Those blah canvas shoes don't go well with that outfit. What size are you?"

"Ah, six…."

"Perfect!" he turned to one of the shelves of shoes and grabbed a box. He showed me a brand new pair of pink converse sneaks. "I think you'll enjoy wearing these."

"I couldn't!" I told him.

Just then, the police arrived. The scientist guy ran up to them. "Our robot had a little malfunction."

"Please accept the shoes!" the manager insisted.

"Okay," I said, after all, they were great shoes and the pair I'd secretly been wanting to buy.

He pointed to my feet. "Try them on. I want to make sure they fit perfectly!"

Without even thinking about it, I agreed. After all, I had taken out the robot without much of a fight so I thought my feet would still be fresh. I popped my heel out of my shoe. I popped my toes out. I wiggled them some. I heard a gasp, and then another and another. Then a plop, plop, plop. Within a second I was the only one left standing in the store and as well, in that entire area of the mall! I picked up my shoe and sniffed it. Oops! I had forgotten about nervous sweat! I slipped my foot into the pink converse. On the bright side, it fit perfectly.

I sighed. Rushing back to the bathroom at super speed so no security cameras would notice me. I changed into my regular outfit then headed back to the store and helped revive the people.

By then, Oscar Oranga and the press had arrived.

I heard Oscar saying as the camera rolled, "Oscar Oranga reporting from the Star Light City mall. We were called here to cover an out of control Android. Not the phone, a real android. Super Teen showed up and took the android out. But she also took out the entire store and half the mall with a simple whiff of her feet! Which begs the question, is Super Teen a Hero or a Zero?"

The cameraman scanned to show all the people laying out cold on the floor. The medics had arrived and were starting to bring people around.

I ignored the press and headed over to Krista. I gave her a little nudge. "Krista wake up."

Her eyes popped open. She smiled. "Wow, you missed the most amazing thing!"

I shrugged. "Sorry, my stomach gets really nervous during scary stuff like that."

She shrugged. "That's okay we all can't be Super Teen."

Oscar Oranga plunged a microphone into Krista's face. "Young lady, you were one of Super Teen's victims," he prodded. "How do you feel?"

Krista sat up. She smiled. "I feel great. Super Teen saved us all from that crazy HAR robotic-dude thing. It was awesome!"

Oscar waved the mic in front of her. "You don't mind that she knocked you silly? Reviewing footage from the store's security camera shows a simple whiff of her foot downed the entire store!"

Krista's eyes popped open. "Nah, it was the most relaxing thing I've ever experienced."

I stood there in amazement as almost everybody that Oscar Organa interviewed, agreed with Krista. They were scared of the android and grateful that Super Teen had saved them. They didn't mind being put to sleep because in today's hectic world a little nap now and then was a good thing. Even Chief Michaels noted that while he doesn't fully approve of super vigilantes, he appreciated the effort Super Teen made, and that was the best rest he'd had in years.

I couldn't be sure if Oscar liked what he was hearing. When the camera stopped rolling I approached him.

"So, Super Teen is a hero?" I asked.

He looked at me with open eyes and a fake smile. "I guess she is."

I figured I should leave that comment well enough alone. Krista bought her shoes and we headed home.

Dear Diary: Sometimes I forget how powerful I truly am. It's both super cool and super frightening at the same time. To be able to beat a robot up with one hand and then drop an entire store and most of the mall with a whiff of my foot is crazy! I need to be careful though. I love my new converse shoes but I'm so glad nobody actually died.

Still not sure what to make of this reporter dude. I'm starting to think he might feel it's a better story if Super Teen is a menace. I hope I'm wrong. Cause Super Teen can do a lot of good.

I think I need to look out for him or he might be the death of my reputation.

Not So Social Media...

I walked Krista home to make sure she got there safely. She seemed a little loopy after getting a whiff of my feet. A couple of times, I had to put a hand on her back to steady her.

She smiled at me, "You're such a good friend, Lia."

"You sure you're okay?" I asked when we got to her front porch.

She nodded. "I feel fine. I don't know what Super Teen did but that was the most relaxing sleep I've had since I was a kid. I dreamt I was floating on a cloud."

"So, the smell of her feet didn't make you want to throw up?" I asked.

Krista laughed. "No, actually. Her feet were very *overpowering*, but it was kind of in a good way. It made me understand that she really is WAY powerful, but we have nothing to fear. She'll always protect us!" She pointed to her door. "It's been such a fun shopping adventure, but I think I'd better get to my homework."

"Yes, me too," I agreed as I glanced at my watch and realized the time. "See you at school tomorrow, Krista." I smiled at her and waved goodbye.

Part of me felt good that by knocking people out with my slightly stinky feet, made them feel safe. But another part of me found that very weird and a little creepy. That's a lot of power for a young teen to have.

On my way home, I pulled out my phone to check my social media. Sure enough, it had been blowing up, most of it about Super Teen. And the reviews were mixed. There was even a hashtag now...#SUPTEENHERO

I had channel 13 news and Oscar Oranga to thank for that. At least that hashtag gave me the chance to easily see everything that everyone said about Super Teen.

Some people defended me. The defenders were led by Jason; or as he was known on Instagram…@COMICLOVERJ

@COMICLOVERJ: #SUPTEENHERO is a hero, she saved the shoe store from a crazy mad android!

@WENDI: Is #SUPTEENHERO really a hero? She didn't have to knock out the entire store to stop the android. She did it on purpose to show her power. That was dangerous.

@KRISTA: I was there, it wasn't bad at all. I'm glad #SUPTEENHERO saved us. When I came too, I felt better than ever!

@WENDI: Krista…that's because #SUPTEENHERO probably has some weird whammy power that warps your brain.

That conversation went back and forth. Just like any other argument on Instagram or Facebook that nobody ever won. Everybody thought the same at the end as they did in the beginning. I sighed. Most of the other remarks went from either…"She's so cool!" or "She's a threat!" It seemed people were 40 / 60 in support of Super Teen. I smiled when I saw that. Brandon actually questioned Wendi about her comment. I had to admit, it was crazy when I watched everybody drop. Most of them hit the floor before my shoe did. Of course, the excitement was instantly followed by terror and me thinking *OMG I can't believe I did that. I hope they're all ok!*

Dear Diary: I'm so glad Krista and everybody else in the store is okay. And I'm so glad I stopped that crazy HAR…kind of worried that the people my dad works for were behind all that. But I'm more worried about how people feel about Super Teen from now on. I only want to help others, use my powers for good, make the world a better place. I'm starting to figure out some people will support me no matter what. But some people hate change and Super Teen represents change. Those people won't accept change no matter what. Words won't change them but maybe, just maybe, my actions will.

Family Ties...

I got home and found Mom sitting in the living room with Grandma Betsy and Great Grandma Ellen. Man, the three of them could pass as sisters. They had a computer open and were skyping with Great, Great Grandma Ann. She'd moved to the Andes mountains in Peru, so people wouldn't get suspicious of how little the Strong women aged. In fact, Grandma and Great Grandma now even said they were sisters.

"Looks like you've had a busy day!" Mom said as I entered the room.

I saw on the TV they were watching the Channel 13 news. It was showing the people in the store all falling over. Of course, they had the hashtag: #SUPTEENHERO Underneath the picture. The headline sticker had such interesting updates:

-BM Science regrets Android HAR's actions, will give the school new cleaning Androids

-Mayor TJ Bass undecided if Super Teen is a threat

-Police Chief Michaels Claims he welcomes the help but is cautious

-Store Manager thankful for the help and that nobody got hurt

Grandma and Great Grandma walked over to me and kissed me on the head.

"We came to help you with your family history report," Great Grandma said. "We even have my mom online so she can chip in her knowledge. The woman did fight in a world war, after all."

Grandma gave me a strong hug. "Of course we are here to talk about your powers as well. That's if you want to."

I sat down on the couch so I could see into the

computer screen and waved to Great, Great Grandma. "Hi GGG!" I said. That's what I'd always call her. Now, of course, it finally made sense why I had so many grandmas and they all still looked great.

"Hi, kiddo!" GGG said.

I sighed and knocked over the computer on the table. "Oops, sorry!" I giggled.

The grandmas laughed. "Just growing pains." Grandma Betsy said.

"Can I take my shoes off?" I asked them. "These things are a little tight."

"Sure," Great Grandma Ellen said.

I kicked my shoes off. Mom and Grandma Betsy were sitting beside me. They both coughed a little.

"That is pretty powerful," Grandma Betsy said.

Mom nodded. "Yeah, that nervous sweat. It can have quite a kick."

Great Grandma Ellen sat directly across from my feet. Her eyes seemed to be spinning in her head. I wiggled my toes without thinking. She slumped back over on the couch.

"Wow!" Mom said.

"Super impressive!" Grandma Betsy said.

"I didn't expect that!" I said.

"She'll come around in a minute or two," Grandma Betsy assured me. "You just caught her off guard. She wasn't prepared for that kind of power."

"Am I that powerful?" I gulped.

Mom and Grandma shrugged. "Apparently, but you'll figure it out with time."

Great Grandma Ellen started to stir. She sat up. "Impressive young lady!" she smiled. "Very relaxing nap!"

I shook my head. "Yeah, I don't get that. Why do people I knock out with my foot odor seem so happy afterward?"

"Sounds like your pheromone power is developing," Mom explained, sounding like a scientist.

"Pheromones are a scent that people give out to make themselves more attractive to others," Grandma Betsy added.

"Right, I remember Mom telling me about them."

Grandma Betsy smiled. "Trust me, honey it's a great ability to have. Once you get control of it, you'll be able to help control any situation. Plus it's fun. One time I was presenting a demonstration about a product that the company I worked for were trying to sell. I was in front of about 100 people. But there was a very rude man in the audience, calling out and embarrassing me in front of everyone. So, I made him think he was a pussy cat and he

44

started meowing. Then he fell asleep in his chair! Everyone started laughing at him. It was a crack up!"

"Oh my gosh! So it's like hypnosis?" I asked.

Mom shook her head. "No, with hypnosis you can't make people do things they wouldn't normally do. With pheromones, you can."

"Wow," I said. "Another scary power."

Great Grandma Ellen grinned at me. "It's just another tool in our kit."

"You're so brave," GGG said, "being the first one of us to openly use your powers in public!"

I dropped my head. "Not sure if it's brave or silly!"

Grandma Betsy put her arm around me. "Definitely brave!" she said.

I gave them a weak smile. "Thanks!"

Mom looked me in the eyes. "What else is on your mind honey?"

I hesitated. "Well, I hate the fact that I have to give an oral report on family history and what the 1960s, 1970s, 1980s, and 1990s were like."

Mom shook her head. "Yeah, public speaking can be scary. But I think there's something else on your mind."

"Spit it out, girl!" GGG said from the computer screen.

I tossed myself back on the couch. "I'm worried that other friends or enemies might figure out I'm Super Teen. I mean my costume isn't that fancy. Or tricky. I don't even wear glasses like Clark Kent in Superman. Not only do I not need them but they'd look so bad on me. I'd love to do something extra to add to my disguise."

My two grandma's looked at each other. Grandma Betsy slid behind me. She took my hair gently in her hands and pulled it into two bunches at the sides of my head. "Your hair will look so good like this. And because you never wear it this way, it'll help to disguise you. Plus, it's easy to put up like this!"

Grandma Ellen held a mirror up for me.

I had to admit I did look different. For some reason, I never wore my hair tied up, and it seemed to change my look completely.

"Any other questions about being super?" Great Grandma asked.

I nodded. "Well, how come these powers just kick in when we turn 13?"

Grandma put a hand on my shoulder. "Easy dear, our bodies require at least 4745 days to absorb the energy they need to charge our cells."

"Wow!" I said. "That's a lot of days in just 13 years. I never thought of it like that."

We spent the next few hours chatting about the history of the Strong family and how life has changed over the decades as well as how it has remained the same. I learned that before the Strong women came to the US, we were mostly found in Great Britain. Great Grandma thought maybe the Scotland area. Grandma thought Ireland. GGG thought Wales. The point being, the records back then were very thin. All we could determine was that we had ancestors from all over that area. I wondered if any of them were related to King Arthur or maybe even Merlin. Not sure why my mind just goes off track like that sometimes. But it's fun.

Mom must have noticed my mind was wandering as she gave me a little nudge to bring me back to the moment. "I understand this report will be half your grade for this semester," she prompted.

"I didn't tell you that," I said. In fact, I hadn't known that.

"Jason did," Mom said. "He thought I should remind you," she smiled.

"I like that Jason boy," he has potential, Grandma Betsy said.

"He's nice," Great Grandma Ellen said slowly. "But he's just so normal."

"Normal is good!" GGG Ann chimed in via the computer.

Great Grandma Ellen smiled. "Now that Brandon fellow! He's a catch. He's strong, a leader, smart and hot!"

"Great Grandma!" I shouted, feeling my face turn red. It sounded so weird to hear her talk like that!

Her smile grew. "Hey, I may be old but I still know hot when I see it." She paused for a moment, took a breath then added, "A Strong woman needs a strong man."

"Give the girl time, Mom!" Betsy said to Ellen. "She just turned 13!"

"When I was 13, I was dating a senior, in college!" Great Grandma Ellen grinned, "But of course he thought I was 18."

"A couple of us back in the day were married at 14," GGG chimed from the computer. "Not that I would advise that…. Just saying…"

"Can we please change the topic back to history?" I begged. For once, I really wanted to talk about history. Nothing more embarrassing than having my grandmothers talk about my "relationship" status, or lack of a "relationship" status.

Mom spoke up to help me out. "Great Grandma can you tell us about life in the 1950s?" she asked.

For the next couple of hours or so, my three grandmas and my mom told me about life since the 1950s. It was then up to me to figure out what was alike and what was different, to life nowadays.

Halfway through, I began to get really hungry, so we ordered pizza and wings and got one pizza with garlic and onions. Let me tell you, after eating that, the four of us could have dropped an army with our breath. And wow, it wouldn't have even been a close fight. GGG Ann kidded she could smell our breath over the computer.

Before winding up our discussion, Grandma Betsy had one more suggestion to help with my oral presentation.

"Just pop your heels out of your shoes before you talk! Your pheromone power will make sure they all love it!"

"Mom!" my mother said.

Grandma Betsy looked at Mom. "Now, Isabel you can't tell me you've never used your pheromones...."

Mom crossed her arms. "Mom! This isn't about me." She looked sternly at me. "I know you'll do what's right!"

I nodded and gave her a weak smile.

She walked over to me and gave me a big hug. "You might have only just developed your super powers, but as far as I'm concerned you've always had the power! Lia, your presentation will be a smash hit. You have nothing to worry about!"

I gulped nervously. Something told me, that it was not going to be quite that easy.

Dear Diary: Amazing! All my grandmas are so alike and yet so different! I love each one of them. I'm glad now I finally understand why I have them all in my life. They were a great help to me tonight. There are some things you rely on friends for but other things you need family to help you with. I also have to admit that I liked Grandma Betsy's idea of giving the class a little blast of my foot power. Not enough to drop them all, but enough to make them listen to my every word in awe.

But then I shook off that idea. For one it was wrong, I can't use my powers to make my friends do what I want. Yeah, it would be cool, but it's not what a hero does. Plus, with my luck and lack of control, I might knock out the entire school. That just wouldn't be good, and awful hard to explain anyway. Besides I was given this power for a reason. I want to help leave my mark on the world. I have an opportunity to make the world a better place. I can help those who can't help themselves. Oh my gosh, I'm so strong I can even help those who can help themselves. What I'm trying to say (and not doing a great job of), is that I want to make the world better. By better, I mean better for everybody, not just for me. Mom always says, "Competition is fine, but people accomplish great things when they cooperate." Now that I have this power, I finally get what Mom means. I could change the world, but not just as Super Teen, also as Lia Strong. My personality is as strong as any of my powers.

Okay, now I'm rambling on and getting a bit carried away. I get like this from time to time. Maybe I should nab more of that pizza? OMG! Why am I writing this down?

Another New Kid in Town?

Jason played it pretty smart during our walk to school on Monday. He was being very tactful and didn't even bring up the fact that I knocked out an entire store and part of the mall with super foot odor.

Instead, he focused on our assignment. "How's the report coming along?"

"I feel much better about it now that I've talked with my grandmas," I replied. "I'm still nervous as anything about talking in front of the class, but at least I now have some good things to talk about."

Giggling, I continued, "One of them even suggested that I pop my shoes off before I talk, just to put everybody to sleep and then get them to love what I'm saying."

"Okay, I'm not sure what to make of that," Jason answered slowly. Hesitating for a moment, he continued, "Do you want to talk about what happened at the mall?"

I nodded, slightly embarrassed.

We were in front of Ms. Jewel's house. Her mean and nasty Doberman, Cuddles, began to run towards us. The dog stopped and sniffed the air. Then he turned and ran back into the house, tail between his legs. Ms. Jewel just waved to us from her porch. "Have a good day at school, kids!"

Jason and I waved back and kept walking, as that had become our new normal way of dealing with big fierce Cuddles, who realized it was me and then becoming a scared little puppy. It felt both good and weird at the same time.

"Yes, yes I do want to talk about what happened at the mall," I nodded. "I need to talk it out with a friend."

Jason smiled. "I think it's really cool, as long as you

can learn how to control it."

I nodded again. "Yes, I'm working on it."

"How do YOU feel about it?" Jason asked, curiously.

"On one hand, it feels great knowing I have this power. I stopped that HAR easily. I loved it. On the other hand, I'm a little worried that part of me got a tiny bit excited about knocking the store out so easily. I could have had an awesome shopping spree and taken whatever I wanted. Nobody could have stopped me." I noticed my heart pounding and I was forced to take a couple of breaths to calm myself.

Jason smiled at me. "Lia, you stopped yourself from doing that. And that's what's important. It's only natural that you would question your power and want to experiment to see what you can do with it. We all have thoughts that are less than good now and then. It's part of human nature I guess. Apparently, super human nature is no different."

"How'd you get so smart?" I asked him.

"You have feet that can can drop a team of ninjas. I have brains!" He smiled.

"I'm smart too!" I said giving him a little shove.

"Yeah, I have to agree with that, I guess," he grinned back at me.

"Hi, Lia! Hi, Lia's friend!" Felipe shouted from across the street. He stood waiting for the school bus. A short older blond kid stood next to him. It was nice the kid seemed to be looking out for Felipe. But that kid gave me a weird chill.

"Hi, Felipe!" I shouted back with a wave. "Hi, Felipe's friend!" I added.

Jason just waved.

We kept walking. "Do you know who the older kid with Felipe is?" I asked.

Jason nodded. "He's Felipe's older cousin Tomas. For some reason, he's staying with them for a while."

"Why doesn't he go to school with us?" I asked.

Jason shrugged. "I think he's home schooled."

"How do you know everything?" I asked.

Jason shrugged again. "When you have open ears and eyes and your dad is police chief, you learn stuff."

I grinned at Jason. I loved that our relationship hadn't changed. It remained nice and normal.

Just then I heard in my mind, *"You're different girl!"*

Okay, so much for normal. I didn't know where that thought had come from. Or if I'd really heard it at all.

Jason looked at me curiously. "What's wrong?" he asked, a worried expression suddenly appearing on his face.

I shook my head. "I think I heard something in my head….it said…" I whispered to him, "You're different girl!"

Jason patted me on the shoulder. "That's probably

just your subconscious talking to you. Letting you know you *are* different. Which you are... but different is good."

"You sure?" I asked, eyebrows raised.

"Of course I am, I got an A on my psychology report last year!" He grinned.

"Oh yes, that makes me feel SO much better," I told him.

When we finally approached the school building, Tony spotted us and held the door open as he waited for us to enter. "Come on you two, let's not be late for home room," he prompted. Since I'd put Tony in his place last week, he'd been so nice to us both.

"Thanks, Tony," I said.

"Wait, no tip?" he asked.

I turned to look at him. He took a step back and grinned. "Just kidding you. My friends get into the school for free!"

"Tony, everybody should be let into the school for free," I lectured.

He smiled and opened up his arms. "Of course they should, because they're all my friends! Now come on. Let's get to homeroom. We don't want to be tardy..."

I grinned. I got the school bully to hold the door open and use the word tardy. Yeah, being super might have its bad points but overall, being super was well, super. Sure, I had a strange voice in my mind. But I decided to take Jason's advice and ignore it. After all, who better to give psychology advice than a 13-year old who got an A on his paper?

Dear Diary: Jason is a great friend. I often wonder if he might be more than that someday. I kind of hope so. But I also kind of worry about that too. What if we broke up? I'd lose his friendship. That would crush me.

Oh, that Tomas kid gives me the creeps. Hard to believe he's related to cute little Felipe.

Bot rot...

As we walked towards our lockers, we saw Janitor Jan being trailed by a hovering domed robot with big white brushes on its bottom. A woman in a white lab coat and holding an iPad followed them both. The woman's lab coat had a BM Science logo on it. Looking closely at the robot, I saw that it too had the BM Science logo. Well, I had to give BM Science credit for being persistence. The mayor, TJ Bass, a big tall gawky guy with curly hair, had previously come to our school and given us all a little speech. "We welcome the addition of this cleaning robot and thank BMS for their contribution. They truly want to help make Starlight City a better place."

At the time, we had all clapped politely. Then the mayor headed out to what I could only guess would be another short, meaningless speech somewhere else.

And now it seemed, the new addition was in action at our school. I wondered what Janitor Jan thought of it. I guessed she was probably worried that a robot would end up taking over her job. I watched as it cleaned the floor around the lockers.

Marie and Lori had just arrived at the locker area as well. Their attention turned to the robot as it used a laser beam from its dome to clean a spot on the floor.

"Not sure if that's cool or over kill!" Lori said.

Marie shuddered. "I don't like it," she said

The BM Science lady overheard them and commented, annoyed at their reaction. "I assure you this cleaning robot is 100% effective."

"Like the home aide robot in the mall yesterday?" Tim asked. He and Krista had just arrived as well. Tim pointed at Krista. "It scared my poor friend here!"

Krista dropped her head. "It only scared me a little."

The BM Science person rolled her eyes. "I'm sure the robot would have deactivated if that annoying Super Teen hadn't stepped in and destroyed it! That cost us a ton of money."

"See! Super Teen is a menace!" Wendi exclaimed, leaning on her locker. "Plus, she doesn't wear cool outfits at all! I don't know what everyone is going on about!" she added with a smirk.

Brandon seemed about to say something, but Wendi cut him off with a look. I like to think that Brandon is on my side. Well, the side of Team Super Kid.

"Yeah she is dangerous," Lori agreed. "But gotta love her power!"

"I think she tries to help!" Marie said.

Wendi zoomed in on Krista. "Krista you were there at the mall when it happened. Didn't she knock you out with her super foot odor?"

Krista frowned. "Yeah, I was there, and yes she put me to sleep, but it was by accident."

Wendi shook her head. "Well, that's even worse than doing it on purpose!"

A couple of kids nodded and grunted in agreement. I decided to stand back and see how this played out. Jason got ready to jump to my defense, but I squeezed his arm preventing him. I didn't need him to seem too eager.

"The thing is," Krista said slowly, "I don't think it was the smell that hit me. I just felt overwhelmed by her raw power."

A couple of the kids, Tony being one of them, seemed impressed by that.

Wendi, of course, was not. "That doesn't make it any better to me."

"You wouldn't understand," came a voice from the back of the crowd. Jessie came forward. "Face it, Wendi, you have a very limited understanding of the world."

"Who do you think you are?" Wendi asked, making a fist and heading towards Jessie. Jessie held her ground.

The always calm Brandon stopped Wendi by grabbing her arm and pulling her back. "Wendi, don't worry about it," he said. How could she not calm down with him at her side? "I don't think Jessie meant anything by it."

Jessie shrugged. "Well, you've been in Starlight City all your life so you see life through a very narrow lens; which is fine. You just need to accept that you don't know everything. In fact, you don't know much at all. You'll be happier when you do." Jessie walked by Wendi and Brandon and into the classroom.

Wendi opened her mouth to say something, and all eyes locked on her. But instead of speaking, Wendi sneezed. "Achoo! Achoo!! Achoo!!!"

Everybody cracked up, even Brandon. Wendi glared at us all. "Sneezing is not funny!"

Brandon hugged her. "Yeah, that was kind of funny, especially with the timing!" he insisted.

Before any of us could say anything else, the bell rang

announcing the start of a new school day. I guess both Wendi and Jessie were literally saved by the bell. Jessie certainly had a different way about her. I liked that!

The rest of the school day actually went fairly normal, at least as normal as middle school can ever get. I found morning science class pretty interesting. After spending the last couple of weeks on the planets, this week we started talking about space travel. Mr. Ohm's little round face lit up when he talked about the future of man in space. We started learning about rockets, and how it was so important for them to be launched with enough energy to escape Earth's pull of gravity. This was necessary in order to break past Earth's atmosphere into space.

For a while, I actually even forgot that I was super. That was until lunch when I was forced to pass on the baked beans. Even before I was super, those weren't a favorite. Now, they were a definite 'No.' I wasn't even sure why the cafeteria offered those.

Jessie sat with us at lunch again. She mostly read a book called Watership Down. But if we asked her a question she would answer it with either a polite yes, or no, or maybe. Tim thought that meant she was warming up to us. I noticed Wendi shooting Jess the evil eye all through lunch. That was until the entire cafeteria cracked up when Bobby Parker slipped on a banana peel and spilled his chocolate milk all over Wendi. Wendi screamed and threatened to have poor Bobby banished from the school. But Brandon told her being school President didn't give a person that power. Plus, Brandon pointed out that Bobby was a good guy who had just slipped and slips do happen.

I caught Jessie smirking through the entire event. She might have seemed cool and aloof but she paid attention to what went on around her. A weird part of me started to wonder if Jessie had anything to do with the run of bad luck that was happening to Wendi. Nah, that's impossible. Right? Of course, until last week I thought it would be impossible for me to lift a moving car off the ground like it was a toy car, and to drop a room full of people by popping off my shoe. So, I guess really anything could be possible. Like Great Grandma always said, "The world is a random wonderful crazy place!"

In History, Mr. P reminded told us that we had until midweek to finish the oral part of our projects. The entire class groaned and moaned. I did too. We thought we'd have until the end of the week at least. Mr. P explained that because we each need to speak for ten minutes, the only way he could make this work was to bring the deadline forward a bit. Each day, starting on Wednesday, he would randomly draw five names from a hat and those five people had to be ready to present their oral project. The paper to go with the project would still be due next Monday. He apologized to us but then pointed out that life often changes the rules as it goes along.

Wendi raised her hand and even offered to go first since she was already organized. She said that because she had such an awesome family the report had been easy. Mr. P thanked her but told her he'd still use the hat, although it was good that she was ready. Wendi knew he'd say that; she just wanted to brag about her family and already being prepared.

The rest of the school day happily passed by without any problems. A big kid, Ryan Taylor accidentally bumped into me, and I had the good sense to fall down. I wanted to make sure nobody even got a hint that I was Super Teen. Yep, I was pretty proud of that.

All in all, the day went well. Of course, that couldn't last. As I stood at my locker after school preparing for LAX practice, I heard a scream.

"Hey, you crazy robot. Stop that! Stop that now!"

Then in a robot tone: "You have dirt on your buns, therefore I must clean it!"

ZAPP!!!!

"Ouch!! You crazy robot!"

I rushed towards the commotion. I saw the cleaning robot hitting Janitor Jan in the buns with a red beam of energy. The BM Science person ran behind the robot saying stuff like:

"Stop!"

"Abort!"

"Humans aren't dirt!"

The crazy robot (a phrase I've been using a lot lately) didn't listen. It hit Jan with another blast. Jan swatted the robot with her mop.

"Ha! It will take more than a cleaning device to stop me!" the robot taunted.

"Yeah, but how about a LAX stick!" Lori yelled.

Lori and Marie launched themselves at the crazy robot. Marie hit it over the dome with her stick! Lori threw a shoulder block at the robot. She hit it hard. But the robot bounced off her.

"Better than a mop!" the robot admitted. "But still not enough to harm me!"

I had to stop this robot. But I had to do it in a subtle way. Lori and Marie had it distracted as they whacked it with their sticks, but that wouldn't hold it for long. I thought about using heat vision, but that might be noticed. The last thing I needed now was people seeing heat coming out of my eyes, and then realizing what was going on. I didn't believe I was even considering this, but it may very well be a time for super spit. Yep, super spit. Not lady like at all, but it could work.

I rolled my tongue around my mouth to collect some spit. I aimed. I blew out a little wad of spit! The spit hit the robot in the midsection, breaking through the robot's metal shielding. The robot crumbled to the ground.

Lori and Marie raised their sticks in victory. I felt good for them. I also felt great that I'd saved the day even though nobody else knew it. I had used my brains to use my powers in a secretive but effective way!

Dear Diary: So now this is normal in my life, defeating robots that have gone mad. Well at least nobody can say I have a boring life. I take pride in knowing I took the crazy bot down very intelligently without anybody knowing I did it! Gotta admit I did miss a bit of the praise and awe from other people, but I didn't miss the haters on social media pretty much saying Super Teen isn't all that great at all. BTW, social media loved that Marie and Lori took out the robot and saved Janitor Jan. Sigh (yes I wrote sigh). I guess normal kids doing heroic things are easier for people to deal with than Super Teen doing something heroic. I need to remind myself that I am Lia Strong. Super Teen is just a small part of my personality and not a defining part. Super Teen is a tool for me to get things done while still leading a normal life as Lia.

I talked to mom about that weird message I had heard in my mind. She told me that it was either 1) I was over tired 2) it was absolutely nothing 3) it was another super being trying to communicate with me.

Mom did hint that there may be other advanced or supernatural beings around. She had never met any, but that didn't mean they couldn't or wouldn't exist. She told me, and I quote, "It's impossible to prove a negative." When I asked her to explain she said it meant you can't prove something doesn't exist. The universe is always expanding.

So who knows?

A different kind of kid...

During the next couple of days, life was pretty boring. But boring can be good. Boring lets you recharge and energize for the not so boring times, the times when you need all your wits and strength. I was glad that Super Teen could take the time off and let me deal with just being Lia.

I put the finishing touches on my paper and oral report about my family history. My heart pounded on Wednesday when Mr. P pulled the lucky names from the hat and announced who would go first: Carol Lester, Vanesa LeBlan, Meghan MacKenzie and Buddy Jason.

I gotta say they all did way better than I could. Sure, they were probably the four smartest kids in the class (kind of weird how that happened), but they seemed to hold back any nervousness they had. Later, Jason told me the secret of public speaking was to picture everybody in their underwear, as it would help you to relax. Not sure I wanted to do that.

Walking home, we noticed Felipe being met at the bus by his cousin, Tomas. Felipe gave us an enthusiastic wave. Tomas gave us a polite nod. We decided to go over and introduce ourselves to Tomas. After all, being a new kid in town, he probably wanted to meet people.

"Hey, Felipe we thought we'd come over and chat with you and get to meet your cousin, Tomas a bit!" I said.

Felipe smiled. He stood there with his legs crossed. "Ah, ah great," he said. "But I have to rush to the bathroom now! I'll leave you guys to talk!" He leaped into the house.

"Well, thank you for coming over," Tomas said, not looking either of us in the eye. "It's hard meeting people when you're home schooled. Plus, I'm kind of shy. Even when I go to the public library I sit in the basement. It's quiet there, just me and my books. Well, not *my* books, but a bunch of books for me to read. I love books."

"I do too!" I said.

"I think we all love books," Jason said. "But why don't you go to the public school?"

Tomas looked up at him. "My family insists I am special. Too special for public schools!"

Okay, I got the impression Tomas didn't want to talk about this. But Jason, for all his brains, wasn't always the best person at picking up on somebody else's vibes. He pushed the matter. "You know, Starlight City Public Schools have a great reputation."

Tomas laughed. "That sounds like something Mayor TJ Bass would brag."

"Perhaps, but it's still true!" Jason said. "We get an excellent education and we get to hang out with our friends."

I love Jason, but he could be such a dense geek at times when dealing with new people.

"Really?" Tomas said.

"Really!" Jason said.

Tomas crossed his arms. He looked at Jason. "I bet you don't even know how many moons Mars has?"

"Sure I do, one hundred!" Jason said. "Wait, that's not right."

"I know you don't know the Pythagorean Theorem!"

Jason stomped a foot down. "A something equals CAT!" he said.

"Ah Jason, that's not right! Not even close," I told him. Something weird was going on here.

"Let's do an easy one. I know you can't spell cat!" Tomas taunted.

Jason gave him a confident wave. "Oh please, that's so easy! I'm not even going to tell you!" he said, with a bravado in his voice I hadn't ever heard from Jason.

"You can't do it!" Tomas laughed.

I turned to Jason. "Jason, you can spell…cat!"

Jason nodded. "I can but I won't!" he said, taking a step away from me.

This was very unusual behavior from Jason.

"Show us how you spell CAT!" Tomas ordered.

Jason spoke slowly like he really didn't want to, "C – A – N!" He said.

"Jason, he means CAT like the animal!" I said.

"Right!" Jason said, standing up straight. "I got this…"

"No, you don't!" Tomas grinned.

"K-A-T!" Jason said proudly.

Tomas laughed.

"Well, it was close," I said, patting Jason on the shoulder.

Tomas shooed Jason away. "Skip along home now so the smart people can talk!"

"Right boss!" Jason said. He turned and skipped across the street.

I curled my hands into fists. I showed Tomas my fists. "Listen, buddy, I don't like people playing with my friends like that!"

Tomas took a step back, eye brows raised. "Calm down!" he said. "Just having a little fun. You like fun!"

I took a step closer to him. "I will not calm down!" I shouted. The force of my voice sent him reeling backward.

Tomas held up both hands for me to stop. "I knew you smelled different!" he said.

"What?" I said storming towards him.

"Don't get me wrong, you smell fine. Just way more powerful than normal humans. I knew you were her. But when you didn't respond to my mental message I thought maybe I was wrong."

"So you're the one who tried talking in my mind?"

Tomas nodded. "I didn't try. I did talk to your mind. You just didn't respond. Not my fault."

I rolled my eyes. "It kind of was, since I had no idea what was going on!"

Now Tomas rolled his eyes. "I thought being super, you'd figure it out!"

I put a finger to my mouth. "Sssh, don't say that out loud!"

Tomas smiled. "Don't worry! We can talk privately, anybody within listening distance is asleep on their feet right now." He smiled. "It's amazing, but my powers don't work on you!"

I stopped and looked around. Mrs. Spring who had been weeding her flower bed had her eyes closed. A couple of kids playing tag stood there asleep. Mr. Pool slept as he held a hose and watered his grass. You could hear the snoring from here.

"What are you?" I asked.

Tomas held out his hand. "Tomas Richards, half-vampire at your service ma'am!"

"Half-vampire?" I asked.

"On my mom's side," Tomas answered, as though this was a perfectly normal thing.

"What does being a half-vampire mean?"

Tomas got excited. "It means I can go out in the sun and I don't care about blood. I can make simple minds do what I want them to do. And I'm way strong!" He smiled. "Once on a camping trip, I ran into a grizzly bear. He growled at me. I farted at him. I used him as a foot rest for the rest of the trip."

"Ah cool, I guess..."

Tomas looked me in the eyes. "Don't worry, I didn't do any real damage. I just showed him who's boss. Like you did to that herd of cattle."

I put a hand over my chest. "What? Me?"

Tomas laughed. "Oh come on! I know victims of a super fart when I see them on the news. Not that I've ever seen them before. That's why I asked my mom if my aunt could home school me for a bit. I wanted to meet you. It's hard being super and not having somebody to share being super with, who is your age."

"I know the feeling," I sighed. My sigh pushed him back some.

"Wow! You *are* powerful!" he said, eyes popping open.

"Just be glad I didn't have any garlic today," I added.

He looked at me. "So you want to hang out sometime?"

"I have an idea. Tomorrow, why don't you meet me and the gang at Mr. T's after school? You do eat, right?"

"I do!" Tomas said. "But not sure I should go. I don't do well with normal people."

"I find it's nice to be around regular people," I told him. "I try not to stand out."

"I'm not a big fan of regular people, as you call them," Tomas told me.

I looked him in the eyes. "Trust me, give them a chance!"

Tomas hesitated, then said, "Fair enough. I will meet you there."

"My friend will be okay, right?" I asked.

Tomas grinned. "Yeah, he will. He won't even remember I turned him into a dunce."

"Okay, I have to go now… but I'll see you tomorrow!" I told him.

"Great, I look forward to it!"

"Do you mind if I tell my mom about you? She's super too."

"Go for it!" Tomas said.

I turned towards home, thinking, "OMG! I just met a vampire, well half-vampire." I stopped and turned back to Tomas. "Wait! Does this mean Felipe is a half-vampire too?"

Tomas shrugged. "He is my blood. So you do the math!"

Dear Diary: Never think life can't get any stranger. Now, not only was I super but I was neighbors with a half-vampire teen. A kid who can make people do whatever he wanted and could drop a grizzly with a fart. I could relate.

Mom wasn't shocked at all. She told me she figured if we could be super then there had to be other "non-normal-beings" around. She wouldn't be surprised if more started to show up now that I had kind of presented myself to the public. People were figuring out that supers and normals could live together. I hoped.

Actually, I wanted to make people understand that being super didn't mean a person wasn't normal.

Robots not in disguise...

Thursday started as my most normal day in a long time. No strange things happened in the morning. At lunch, Jessie even answered our questions when we talked to her.

I felt relief again in History class when my name wasn't one of the four picked from the hat. Instead, the cheerleaders, Michelle Noah, and Cindy Kay were picked, along with the debate team captain, Jackson Jacobs. Jessie was also chosen. They all seemed far less nervous than me. Jackson actually spoke for twice as long as required. Michelle and Cindy both spoke with a lot of passion. Jessie's speech was quite deep. She talked about persecution in the past. I guess it's true what Grandma Betsy says, lots of stuff goes on for people that we don't even know about.

The good news was that there were no robot attacks in school. BM Science insisted they had taken all the bugs and defects out and Jan the Janitor actually seemed happy to have the help. As well, I made it to LAX practice without anything abnormal, funky or weird happening.

But of course, that didn't last.

I was having a pretty good practice. First, we ran drills. I actually like drills because I enjoy repetition. There is something comforting about doing something over and over and watching yourself improve.

After that, we scrimmaged a bit. I scored a nice goal where I tucked the ball into the corner of the net above the goalie, Kelly Richard's shoulder. "Great shot!" Krista said, giving me a high five. Marie followed with a fist bump. Even Kelly acknowledged me with a nod of her head.

That's when I heard inside my head:

"*Lia, this is your dad, I'm broadcasting on a frequency only you (and probably your mom and grandmas) can hear. We have a problem at BM Science and we need your help! Over and out,*

Dad."

My first thought was to ignore it. After all, I don't hear from my father in over ten years and now all of a sudden he reaches out to me, just because I'm super. And only because he needs me! But he was my dad. And he did need me.

I smiled, knowing Mr. Coach Blue was our coach today. I guess I should clear that up some. We actually have two coach Blues for LAX. They are a husband and wife coaching team. Normally she coaches us and he coaches the guys, but now and then they switch. And Mr. Blue always took it easier on us than Mrs. Blue.

I walked up to Coach Blue holding my stomach and bending over. "Coach, something I ate at lunch didn't agree with me at all…" I leaned in close to him and whispered, "I think I'm going to vomit…."

Coach put an arm on my shoulder. "Take the rest of the practice off, go home and get some rest."

I dragged myself off the field, holding my stomach. I heard Wendi mumble under her breath, "Wimp…" Couldn't let her bother me now.

I got to the locker room and collected my stuff. Good thing I kept my Super Teen outfit in a bag in my book bag. I also kept a pair of old socks in that bag to stop anybody from looking into it. The smell was even better than a padlock.

A text appeared on my phone.

JASON>My dad has been called 2 BMS…something weird going on.

I text backed> OMW there

I moved into the bathroom, changed at super speed and leaped out the window. I leaped and bounded my way to BM Science, keeping my book bag by my side. After a few minutes of super hopping, the BM Science lab complex came into view. The place was surrounded by a big fence. Police cars lined the gates but the guards at BM wouldn't let them pass.

Using super hearing, I heard Captain Michaels arguing with the guards about how the police had a call regarding an out of control robot. The guards insisted the call was a mistake and shouldn't have been made. My extra super hearing zoned in on people running and screaming in a courtyard beyond the main building. I knew something bad was going down. I stored my book bag in the highest branch of a nearby tree then leaped over the BM Science fence. Another bound and I was on the flat roof of the main building. For a high tech lab or whatever, the building itself looked like a boring white warehouse.

Peering down from the roof to the court and lunch yard below, I could see a big blue robot that looked like a 10-foot-tall robot boxer. People were running in fear as the robot smashed lunch table after lunch table. A couple of security people tried to stop it, but the robot pushed them aside like they were flies.

I saw my dad and a couple of people in lab coats watching from inside the main building. I could see them shaking their heads.

The big blue robot lumbered towards a small blond woman who stood there trembling with fear.

The robot raised an arm and shouted, "I will prove I am the best. I can't be beaten!"

I leaped down between the robot and the woman and caught the robot's arm on the way down before it could smash the lady.

"Not happening on my watch!" I told the robot, as I ripped off its arm.

I felt good about that. The robot reacted fast, way faster than I expected. It swatted me across the face with its remaining arm. That blow sent me staggering back a little.

"Ha! Human! Your fighting is almost as bad as your banter!" It taunted. It swung at me again. This time though, I blocked it. Then I moved forward and hit it with an open palm to its robot stomach. My blow sent it reeling back. The big squared head bot, looked at me and smiled. "Not bad, tiny human!" it said.

The bot took a boxing stance. "I have been programmed to fight!"

I dropped back into a karate stance, "Good, I'd hate to beat up a non-fighting robot!"

"I must warn you, silly human, I have been programmed with every style of fisticuffs and martial arts known to man!"

Okay, I didn't like the sound of that. I had to hope the robot was bluffing. I leaped up, sending a flying kick to the robot's chin. It swatted me to the ground before I got to it. I rolled away as it tried to stomp on me. I bounced to my feet.

The robot laughed, "Ha, I saw that pitiful move coming before you knew you were going to do it!" it shouted.

I pointed at the bot very dramatically, "Your maker must be so proud!"

The robot's stiff face showed a slight smile. "I am not really programmed for emotion or to recognize emotion, but yes I do believe they are."

"Then why are you attacking them?" I asked. I didn't really care, I just needed time to catch my breath and maybe figure out a plan of attack on this big blue bot.

"They wanted me to show them what I can do. So I did. I figured you would show up. I wanted to beat the strongest human in the world!"

I kind of liked being called the strongest human in the world. But now I needed to show this bot what that meant. I just didn't know how. After all, yeah I may have been strong and I might know karate, but I still didn't have a lot of fighting experience. In karate, they never prepare you for facing off against a 10-foot-tall metal robot.

"I see you are using delaying tactics, in order to catch your breath," the robot laughed. "I gave you a sporting chance, but enough is enough." It started running towards me faster than I thought a bot that size should be able to move.

The bot was on top of me before I knew it. It grabbed me with its good arm and lifted me off the ground then threw me down heavily. I rolled up again and noticed a "me" sized dent in the ground.

"Is that the best you've got?" I taunted.

The big blue bot stalked towards me again. "You can take a beating; I'll give you that! I would be impressed except..."

"You're not programmed for emotions," I said.

I leaped up into the air, bounced off a lunch table and sprang up over the bot. I forced myself down, jamming my legs on top of the bot's head. "Like Mario squishing a goomba!" I told the bot.

The bot crinkled but didn't break. Now it was maybe nine feet tall instead of ten. It still had fight in it though. "Figures you'd make a geek reference!"

"Look, if you're trying to taunt me again by calling me a geek, it won't work!" I told the bot. "I'm proud of being a geek!"

The bot let out a chuckle. "Yeah, only a geek would think a pink shirt with green jeans covered in stars, topped off with a black mask would look good!"

"Nope, that won't work either!" I pointed to the outfit. "I know this is cool, plus you have no taste."

"Hmm, then once I take you down I will head to town and knock the town to the ground!" the robot said.

Now that really made me mad! One, I hated the rhyme. And two, no robot was going to threaten my friends and my town. I felt the anger building up inside of me. My eyes began to glow. Beams of red hot heat flew from my eyes into the robot.

The robot exploded with a wondrous BOOM! Robot parts rained down around me. I thought of cold things like eating ice cubes, then blew on the robot parts with icy breath. The robot parts shattered into dust.

I leaped up in the air. I was due at Mr. T's 20 minutes ago!

Vamp Out...

I felt so powerful! Not only had I taken out a crazy robot, my leaps were growing by leaps and bounds. I made it all the way from BM Science to the tree where I'd stashed my book bag in a millisecond. I grabbed the book bag and made another leap. Within a minute, the city had come into clear view. I bounded home, got changed and then headed to Mr. T's.

When I walked into Mr. T's, my mouth fell open. A kid named Jimmy Wall sat there sucking his thumb. Tony, the bully, danced like a ballerina. Mr. T and Mrs. T were asleep on the counter. Jason clucked like a chicken. Marie and Lori played clapping games with each other. Brandon ran around on all fours barking like a dog. He chased Wendi who hissed like a cat. Krista sat at our table but she was sitting on her head. Tim walked back and forth, arms stiff like he was a zombie.

In fact, everybody in Mr. T's was either sound asleep or acting crazily. Well, everybody but Tomas who sat in a chair. The cheerleaders, Michelle and Cindy, massaged his feet. Oh, and for some reason, Jessie sat there at a corner table reading War and Peace.

"Hey, Lia," Jessie said, as I walked by.

I stopped. "You're still you!"

Jessie nodded. "Yeah, the little half-vamp is too smart to try and mess with me," she said.

"Ah, why is that?" I asked.

Jessie pointed to Tomas and the two poor cheerleaders massaging his feet. "Don't you have more important things to do right now?"

"Good point." I turned and headed to Tomas.

"Tomas, what are you doing?" I shouted.

Tomas looked at me. "You're late…"

"Yeah, something came up!"

Tomas pointed over his shoulder to the TV that was showing my fight with the bot. "You look cool!"

"Ssh," I told him.

Tomas grinned. "None of these people can hear anything besides my commands. Well, besides the witch, and she already knows!"

I looked over my shoulder at Jessie. She gave me a wave. "You're a witch??"

Jessie nodded. "Don't fret, I'm a mostly good witch." She pointed at Tomas. "Deal with the issue at hand…"

Shaking my head in disbelief, I looked directly at Tomas, "Why are you doing this?"

"You told me these people were nice and that I could fit in. But when I told them I was a half-vamp, they laughed!" He pointed to the cheerleaders massaging his feet. "Ha! I'm the one laughing now!"

I thought about how to approach this. For one thing, Tomas' feet certainly did smell. I have no idea how Michelle and Cindy were handling it. I pointed to the two poor cheerleaders. "How come they can do that without fainting?" I asked.

Tomas took a sip from a milkshake. "I won't let them faint. This is too much fun!"

I sighed, and my breath knocked Tomas off the chair. The two cheerleaders smiled.

"We're free!" they said.

Then they both passed out on the floor.

"Man, you are strong!" Tomas groaned, standing up.

"Listen, Tomas, these people are nice, or mostly nice, or kind of nice, but they don't take different that easily. You can't just tell them you are a vampire!"

"Half-vampire."

"You can't tell them you are a half-vampire and expect them to believe you, and not think it's a joke, or that you're crazy! That doesn't mean they are bad or unaccepting, they are just used to their world being a certain way."

"But the world changes," Tomas argued.

"Agreed, but we need to ease people into the changes," I told him sincerely.

He pointed to all the people now acting as animals or babies or statues. "Ya gotta admit this is fun!"

"You do have a certain, ah, flare, I'll give you that… but can you make them all normal again?"

Tomas looked at me and frowned.

"Please!" I asked putting my hands together.

"Fine!" he sighed.

I pointed to his shoes. "Oh, put your shoes on first, so they don't all faint after you bring them back to being themselves!"

"Man, you are no fun!" Tomas complained as he slipped his feet into his shoes.

76

He snapped his fingers. "Everybody back to how you were. You don't remember anything about the last ten minutes!"

Everybody snapped back to normal. They all acted like nothing had happened.

"Oh hi!" Krista said to me. "I hope you're feeling better."

"Hey girl, when did you get here?" Tim asked.

Jason came over to our table. "Nice to see you're feeling better!" he told me. He took a bite of a fry. "Why are these cold?"

I sat down. "I invited Tomas to join us today. Since he's home schooled, I thought it would be nice if he got to meet you all!"

Brandon walked by our table, with Wendi close by his side of course. I smiled. Brandon stopped. "You feeling better, Lia?" he asked. I swear his white teeth sparkled almost as much as his eyes.

My face became a giant grin. Brandon had noticed me. "Yes, thanks," I replied, my cheeks flushing with happiness.

Wendi dragged Brandon away. "She's fine, she probably just got a whiff of her own breath. That would make anybody want to throw up!"

"Now, Wendi, that's not nice. Lia smells just fine!"

"Stop smelling other girls!" Wendi ordered.

My group all stared at me as I dropped down in my chair. Trying to take their attention from me, I directed the conversation towards Tomas. "So, Tomas, tell us what you like to do?"

"Do you play any sports?" Tim asked.

"Do you have a girl friend?" Krista asked?

Jason simply rolled his eyes at me. Was Jason jealous of the way I acted around Brandon?

"I like chess and ping pong," Tomas said.

"That's cool!" Tim said with a nod. "We should play

sometime."

"Which one?" Tomas asked him.

Tim took a sip of his milkshake. "Either." He frowned. "Weird this milkshake has turned warm."

Tomas pointed to the TV. My fight was shown on half the screen while Oscar Oranga interviewed people on the other half, asking them what they thought. As always a lot of the people liked me. Some of the people thought I could be dangerous.

"I think she's great!" Jason said.

"I think she's amazing!" Krista agreed.

"I think she's cute!" Tim said.

"She does have a cool look about her!" Krista added.

Tomas took a bite out of a burger. "So you guys aren't scared of her? But she can drop you all with a whiff of her feet."

Krista waved at him dismissively. "Nah, I've experienced that. It's not bad!"

Jason nodded. "That's what I heard too!" He smiled at me.

"Man I wished she'd knock me out!" Tim said. "Then she could give me mouth to mouth!"

"Oh gross!" we all said.

Tim grinned cheekily. Then we all laughed. Even Tomas almost grinned. We sat there for the next hour or so, just munching and talking. Talking about everything, talking about nothing. I believe Tomas even cracked a smile or two.

Around dinner time, Tomas, Jason and I started walking home. Jason asked if I was glad about not having to give my speech yet. I nodded and told him, yes, but I also wanted to get it over with. Tomas said how he loved being home schooled as it was less drama. Jason told him that the drama makes life interesting. Tomas just laughed and said he finds life interesting enough without the drama of school.

I said goodbye to the guys and headed to my house.

"That was fun!" I heard Tomas say in my brain.

"Okay, this is weird!" I thought back.

"Not weird, we're just advanced... Would you go out with me sometime?"

Now that was something I hadn't expected.

"Tomas, I like you but I just want to be friends," I thought back.

"I get it. I'll see you later." He cut his reply short and I didn't hear anything further.

I walked into the house. I hoped he was okay and wasn't upset with me. I guessed it could have gone better. These things always could. Before I could overthink it though, my phone vibrated. Two messages. One from Jason.

JASON> Great job 2day! U were awesome! (muscle)

I texted back: Tnks!

The second message was from my dad.

DR DAD>Thanks for your help, my dear. Love Dad!

Wow! My dad really was back in my life!

Dear Diary: Okay, I'm not sure what the coolest and weirdest moments were with these recent events. Certainly beating up the big blue robot felt great. Once that big blue jerk threatened my town and friends, I knew I had to put him down and hard. I certainly do have a lot of punch! The excitement from that made me tingle all over. But that also showed me how I have to keep my calm. I can't go firing off heat ray vision by accident. Man! That would be bad. Using the freezing breath was, pardon the bad joke, cool.

On the weirder side, Tomas has an interesting way about him. Not sure what freaked me out more, the fact that he could mind control the entire room or how calm he acted. You know it's been a strange day when you find out that one of your new friends is a witch, and that isn't even the oddest part of the day.

Still, the highlight had to be my dad reaching out to me. It's great to have him in my life again. Sure, he summoned me with a mental broadcast but I even found that neat. Sure, he wanted me to defeat a crazy robot. Sure, mom thinks Dad may have been testing my limits. But then he texted me afterward! He told me, good job. I bet he was proud of me. I knew he was. He didn't have to text me. But he did. Yep, my dad was now a part of my life and I liked it.

Oh getting back to the males in my life…it was kind of odd that Tomas would ask me out after only knowing me for a few days. After all, Jason and I have been friends forever and he's never asked me out. Of course, maybe that's why Jason never asked me out, we were such good friends. Whatever! I just hoped I handled it okay. I do want Tomas to be a friend or buddy. You can't have too many friends, and man, he would be a tough enemy. I had to hope for the best. Sometimes even superheroes have to hope for the best. Hmmm…the new normal!

Vamps and Witches, Oh my!...

That evening, I had dinner with Mom and Grandma Betsy. It was a phones off, let's talk and chat dinner, of grilled chicken breast with Mom's gourmet sauce and her special salad. Yum!

"Proud of you for taking out the crazy blue droid!" Grandma Betsy told me. (She was a big Star Wars fan...)

Mom put a hand on my shoulder, "I am too." She hesitated a moment. "Just be careful with your dad... That man always has something up his lab coat sleeve."

I nodded.

"Ah, Isabelle, you just don't like that he always called you Isa," Grandma said with a smirk.

Changing the subject, I asked. "Have either of you dealt with vampires and witches?"

They both shook their heads. "Like I've said before," explained Grandma Betsy, "I've always surmised they existed...but they've stayed hidden away."

"As have we," she added, grinning at me with her eyes as much as her mouth. "You, my dear, have opened up the world to a lot of new things!"

Mom nodded in agreement and I gave them both a weak smile in return. I just hoped opening up the world would be a good thing.

After dinner, I went to my room to do some homework and practice my speech. I worked for about twenty minutes then realized my phone was still off. I turned it back on and texted Jason. I thought for sure, he'd want to chat about my battle with the crazy blue robot.

LIA>How's the night going?

Nothing. I waited a few moments then before sending another text.

LIA>Knock knock!

Still nothing.

A quick check of my social (or unsocial) media showed people once again debating the pros and cons of Super Teen. Surprisingly though, Wendi wasn't complaining about me. She was worried that she hadn't been able to contact Brandon all evening. She'd asked his parents but they didn't seem concerned, and that was strange.

Now was that just a coincidence?

I heard a knock. Not on my door, but on my window; which was extra weird considering I'm on the second floor. Turning to the window, I saw Jessie floating there. I jumped up, opened the window and helped her in.

"Jessie, what's going on?"

Jessie looked around my room. "Hmm, I thought there'd be pictures of pink ponies or unicorns or something. Not LAX posters..."

"I took the unicorns down when I hit 12, but still, a girl can like unicorns, ponies, and LAX as well," I admitted. "But that's not why you are here!"

Jessie shook her head. "No, I figured you might be worried about your buddy, Jason, and the boring perfect looking kid."

"Brandon?"

Jessie nodded. "Yeah that one, he's so blah with his straight teeth and dimples," she stuck out her tongue.

"Jessie, to the point!"

"The half-vamp nabbed them!"

"Why?" I asked.

Jessie shrugged. "Don't know...vamps are weird." She looked me in the eyes. "My guess is he's jealous!"

"What? You're kidding me!" I stared at her. "Do you know where he took them?"

"Kind of," Jessie told me. "I did a locator spell and it showed me Main Street... vamps can be hard to really get a lock on!"

As soon as she said Main Street, I knew where Tomas was keeping them. "The library!" I said. "Tomas said he loves to hang out in the dark basement of the library!"

Jessie smiled. "Vamps can be so cool!"

I headed towards my window. "You coming?" I asked.

Jessie smiled again. "Wouldn't miss it!"

We arrived at the library quickly. Since it was dark I figured I'd handle this as Lia Strong, not Super Teen. After all, this was personal, not heroic. We found one of the library main windows had been forced open. We climbed in the window. It felt kind of freaky being in a dark library. The good thing was that my super sight seemed to see perfectly well in the dark.

The shelves of books made a maze for us to navigate through.

"I'm pretty sure they are in the basement," I said.

Jessie seemed giddy. "This is so cool," she said.

After working our way up an aisle of books and then down a row of books, we found the door to the basement. The door had been smashed open. Pointing at the broken lock, I stated the obvious, "They're down there for sure."

Jessie rolled her eyes. "Wow, brilliant, Sherlock!"

I shot her a look. She took a step back. "Sorry, I can get cynical when I'm excited!"

We made our way down the dark staircase. There, sitting in the middle of the basement was Tomas. He was reading a book by flash light. Tomas sat on top of Brandon and used Jason as a foot rest.

"Oh, so not cool, Tomas!" I said.

Tomas turned to me. I noticed he was reading The Art of War.

He stood up quickly. He staggered. He put his hands behind his back, "Oh, hi. Funny finding you here! This isn't what it looks like!"

"It looks like you've got it in for Brandon and Jason!" I said, thrusting a finger at him.

Tomas dropped his head. "Okay, it is what it looks like then."

I walked over and lifted Tomas off the ground with one finger. "What's your problem?"

"You like them better than me!" he replied.

"Like duh!" Jessie said.

I shot Jessie a look. She backed up a step and said, "Come on now that was obvious as well!"

I let Tomas fall to the ground. I took a deep calming breath. Then another and another. "Look, Tomas, I've known Jason all my life. Well, at least for all of my life that I can remember. He's always been there for me. I've always been there for him. We're great friends. Will we ever be more than that?" I shrugged. "I don't know. Maybe we know each other too well. But whatever there is between Jason and me, has nothing to do with you." I poked him with my finger. "Get it?"

He rubbed the spot where I had poked him. "Yeah, I get it." He motioned with his head towards Brandon, who was kneeling on the floor on all fours. "What about pretty boy?"

"Oh, please, he's Wendi's boyfriend. He's not even interested in me!" I said, my face turning red.

Tomas laughed. "Oh come on! You're smart, you're pretty and you're super powered! Of course, he's interested in you!"

"Duh, again," Jessie said.

A part of me really liked hearing that. Wow!

Another part of me told that part to calm down. I had a lot of flaws...not the least being that one of my farts could drop a town. "Look, Tomas, I appreciate the comments and your feelings... I do...but when I said I'm not ready for a relationship, it has nothing to do with these two guys or with you. You're actually great in your own strange way."

"Thanks. I think," Tomas said.

"Tomas, my life is really weird right now. I have a lot to take in and a lot to learn about myself. I don't want to be more than friends with anybody, not yet. Not until I have a better idea of who I am and my place in this world. This world that gets crazier for me by the day."

Tomas looked at the two guys and ordered. "Get up, walk up the stairs, out the window and go home. If anybody asks, you've been studying late!"

The two boys obediently stood up and walked away.

"Thanks, Tomas," I said.

He shrugged. "Felipe says I have to learn to read human clues better."

"He's a smart kid!" I said.

Jessie came up and put her arm around Tomas. "You know, being a mostly good witch, I'm already aware of my place in this world."

The two of them smiled at each other.

"I'll just leave you two alone!" I said, heading out of there as fast as possible. "Thanks for your help, Jessie!"

"No, thank you!" Jessie told me with a wink.

I smiled then caught up with Jason on the walk home. He was confused. So I thought it best that I made sure he got home safely.

"You know, I have a weird feeling that something really strange just happened," Jason told me, as we reached his house.

I shrugged. "Well, the world is a weird and wonderful place, Jason."

He nodded. "True, but that still doesn't explain why I smell feet?"

Dear Diary: First off, vampires and witches are strange, but in a kind of interesting way. I also have to admit that Tomas

made me begin to come to terms with my feelings about Jason and Brandon, kind of.

The big day...

On Friday morning, I had a feeling of dread. That could only mean one thing. Today would be the day I got chosen to give my oral report. I stayed longer than usual in bed. Shep, our loyal dog, walked into the room. He nudged me with his nose. Shep hated it when I slept late, especially on school days.

I turned to him. "Oh, Shep..." I said. But I couldn't finish, as the second my breath hit him, he whimpered, went, stiff, and fell over. I shot my hand over my mouth. It seemed like my morning breath of death was back. Yeah, that's not ever a good sign of things to come. This showed how unique my life had become. I thought nothing of a whiff of my breath knocking out a 100-pound dog.

After a good teeth brushing and breakfast, Jason and I headed to school. Jason seemed no worse for the events of the night before. He told me he'd had the wildest dreams.

All through the school day, I hoped something would happen that would call for Super Teen to save the day, anything that would give me an excuse to have to leave the school grounds. But of course, when you want a super villain or something to show up, they never do.

Before I knew it, I was sitting in history class. Mr. P probably was the neatest man in the world. He never had a hair out of place. It seemed like his clothing never wrinkled. Not sure why I noticed all of that right then. It's funny the things you pick up on when you're trying not to freak out. Mr. P pulled out a name from the hat, "Lia..."

"Lia who?" I asked grasping at straws.

The classed laughed.

Jason bent over and patted me on the back. "You can do this!"

I stood up. I walked to the front of the class.

"*You can do this, honey!*" I heard Grandma Betsy say in my brain. Not sure how she did that, but it made me feel better. "*Just breathe!*" she mentally coached. "*And don't fart LOL!*" she added. Yeah, she said LOL.

I stood in front of the class. Stay calm, I told myself. My knees started to shake. I felt my palms sweat. I took a breath. I closed my eyes and then I decided to imagine the entire class in their PJs. Somehow mentally picturing Wendi wearing bright orange Sponge Bob PJs put me more at ease. I smiled.

Then I started out talking about how my first ancestors came here in the 1600s. Before that, most of my family lived in the England, Scotland and Ireland area.

"In other words, Great Britain," Mr. P lectured.

I went on to talk about how things have changed. How man has walked on the moon. How today we all walk around with little computers in our pockets that are more powerful than the most powerful computer on Earth at the time man walked on the moon. How the internet has given us all access to unbelievable amounts of information. How these days, the trick is to work out what information is true and what isn't. I talked about how Netflix and Chill were unheard of, not even ten years earlier. I also joked about how my grandma can't wait for her car to be able to drive her to the shopping center of its own accord.

I closed with what I considered the strong point of my talk. "Probably though, the biggest thing I learned doing this project is, the more things change, the more people stay the same. In fact, despite all the technology today and the fast paced life we have, a pace so fast we have to text by leaving out letters or using cool emoticons or LOLs, we are all still much like our ancestors and each other. We all want to be safe and happy. We all want to be part of something larger than ourselves. Rather, we call it a community, a clan, a tribe, a team or a club. We all want to belong and that's because we know things are better when we work together. We all have a role to play! The trick, of course, is finding that role!"

Mr. P gave me a little applause. "Very good, Lia!" I especially loved the conclusion.

When I looked at the class, they all were smiling, even Wendi. Then they all began to applaud as well. I took that as a sign of success.

Before I could soak in the glory for too long though, an announcement came over the PA system. "This is Vice-Principle MacaDoo! The rest of the school day and all after school practices have been canceled. All students and teachers please go to the basement! THERE IS A GIANT ROBOT HEADING TOWARDS OUR CITY!"

Of course, there was!

Mr. P quickly turned on the TV in the classroom. There, stomping towards town, was a giant robot that looked like a huge three story tall square box with long coil legs and five metal arms with claws attached. The police shot at it, but their bullets just bounced off. From the TV we heard Oscar Oranga broadcasting from the street, "This demolition bot has escaped from BM Science's facility. BM says they regret any inconvenience this may cause and they will reimburse people for any damages."

"Quick everybody, to the basement!" Mr. P yelled.

People shot up from their chairs. I rushed over to Jason. "Cover for me!" I said.

"I have your back," Jason told me.

Dear Diary: Speaking in public may be even scarier than fighting giant robots. But I did it!

Bot Battle...

I rushed at super speed through the hallway to grab my outfit out of my book bag.

I heard a mental broadcast from my dad, *"Honey, this robot is nasty. It's meant to bring down sky scrapers, so be careful!"*

Then I heard my mom in my head, *"Since I know I can't talk you out of this, your grandma and I are on the way to lend a hand!"*

"Thanks Mom and Grandma!" I thought back.

"If you need witch help, give me a shout!" Jessie thought to me.

"Thanks all," I thought back at them, as I opened my locker. I grabbed my bag and headed to the bathroom for a quick change.

With everybody moving in the other direction, I had a clear path to the bathroom. Until I saw Vice Principle Macadoo standing in front of the door, that was. I stopped in my tracks. "Ah, sir, I really need to use the facilities," I crossed my legs. "I'm way nervous..."

VP Macadoo was a mountain of a man. He crossed his log sized arms and stood in front of the door. "Sorry, Lia but you have to use the one in the basement. It's safer."

"No, *I'm* sorry!" I said. Okay, I needed to use my pheromone sweat power to convince VP Mac to let me pass. I just had to be careful. I wanted to influence him, not knock him. I knew my feet had to be really sweaty from both the talk and now the nerves of knowing I'd be facing a giant robot. I popped my heel gently out of my shoe, just enough until I got a slight whiff of my foot. Then I quickly popped my heel back into the shoe. VP Mac now had a silly smile on his face.

"You will let me pass!" I said, softly but firmly.

He smiled at me and stepped to the side. "Of course, master!" he answered.

I shook my head. Okay, that was mega odd. "Go down and join the others, and please don't call me master!"

He bowed and headed off.

I super speeded into the bathroom, changed and leaped off to fight a giant robot.

In less than a minute, I had the robot in sight. Following the loud clangs of its feet smashing into the streets, made it easy to track. I landed on the ground maybe a quarter of a mile in front of the giant crazy machine.

The police had the robot surrounded, but their shots, even from heavy weapons, bounced harmlessly off the bot. Mom and Grandma stood behind the police.

"Captain Michaels, have your men stop firing, their shots aren't doing any good against the robot, but they might harm Super Teen!" I heard Grandma command the captain.

"Stop firing, men!" Captain Michaels ordered.

The robot stopped in its tracks. "Ah, Super Teen. I am so filled with joy that you would show up. After all, you are the reason I am here! I want to prove to my makers that I am the most powerful machine or person or animal or vegetable on Earth!"

I bent my knees then sprang forward at the big bad bot. I extended my fist and rammed the bot in the midsection.

I made a little dent.

The bot swatted me to the ground with an open claw hand the size of my body.

I hit the street.

"Oh, that's going to leave a mark!" the bot laughed.

"She can't stop it! Fire men! Fire!!!" Captain Michaels ordered.

The police started raining bullets at the giant bot. The

bullets bounced off the bot's hard metal surface not even scratching it.

"Police, hold your fire! It's useless!" I heard Grandma Betsy order.

"Only Super Teen can stop this thing!" Mom scolded the police.

The hail of bullets stopped.

I rose to my feet. I saw the big "me" sized dent in the

road.

"Told you!" the bot said, thrusting a finger the size of my face in my face.

I swung at the finger with my fist. The bot pulled away. I missed and fell again, face first into the pavement.

"I've been watching you!" the giant white robot gloated. "I know all your moves before you do!" He pointed to his square robot head. "I have a lot of processing power!"

I pushed myself up off the ground and rammed the robot between its legs. The force of my blow lifted it up off the ground. But it thrust itself back down without losing any balance.

The bot reached down with a hand. "If I had been a human male, that attack would have made me at least talk funny," it told me in a high pitched voice. "But I am not!" the bot continued in a trembling roar. Then, it began to squeeze.

I felt pain for the first time since I've been super. A part of me didn't like it at all. But another part of me realized that the pain made me angry. I could use that anger. I pushed out on the robot's hand with my hands and slowly forced the big cold metal hand open.

I shot up! I blasted the bot's head with my heat ray vision. Two intense red beams of sheer power blazed from my eyes into the bot's head. The head turned from white to pink, lost shape and then melted into the body! The bot stood there motionless. The crowd of onlookers cheered!

The top of the bot started to rumble and churn. A new head popped up. "I'm built with the newest and coolest Nano technology. You break something, it repairs itself," the robot laughed.

Oh, this was bad, so so bad. The bot extended a fist over its head. It pounded the fist down at me. I jumped to the side. The fist shattered the road. I leaped backward. The bot struck at me again and again with multiple arms. I retreated, dodging blow after blow. I didn't really have time to think.

"Dad, how could you crazy scientists make such a monster robot?" I asked in my thoughts.

"It's because you've been holding back, honey!" Dad said in my mind.

"What?" I screamed in my head.

"Yeah, what!?" Mom screamed too. It seemed that suddenly I had a conference call going on in my brain.

"Lia, honey, you haven't been really pushing your powers because you've either been afraid of hurting somebody or you haven't been pushed. My team and I have been developing this robot to help you be the best you can be. Exceed the limits you put on yourself!"

The big robot lumbered towards me slowly. He shook his new head. "Oh Super Teen, I had hoped you'd be more of a challenge." Lumbering towards me, it lifted up two of its arms and sniffed. "I haven't even worked up a sweat!" The arms dropped and the robot laughed. "Ha! Ha! Robot humor."

Well, I certainly didn't love the fact that my dad had invented a giant robot just to help push me to be my best. A little part of me thought that was kind of sweet. A bigger part thought, my gosh this is crazy! But I couldn't let this robot hurt my town or my friends. Nope! It was not going to happen! I had to stop this huge humongous thing. I just had no idea if I could. I needed a moment to think and collect my thoughts. Problem was, I didn't have a moment. The bot moved towards me. It's fresh head taunting. "Takes more than you to stop me!"

From behind the robot, I saw Tomas holding up Felipe with one arm. Tomas tossed Felipe like he was a football. Felipe flew towards the giant bot yelling, "Yahoo!"

Felipe hit the robot in the back of the head. The giant robot spun his head around 360 degrees to see what had smacked him. Felipe dropped to the ground next to me.

"Felipe, thanks for the help! But people will recognize

you now!" I told him.

Felipe smiled. "Nah, I have a vampire blur on, regular people just see a weird streak. They have no idea what it is. Silly regular people…"

"Okay, thanks for the little break," I told him.

Felipe streaked back to Tomas.

The robot shook its head and turned back to me. "Now that was hard to compute. What isn't hard to compute is that I am going to clobber you."

"Hey, Lia, this is Jessie broadcasting to you in your brain now. I'm linking you to the thoughts of your friends." I heard a variety of remarks…

Please, Super Teen do this.

I know she won't let us down.

Give him a belting– (that was from Brandon…)

Come on Lia, launch that big ugly bot! (That had to be from Jason!)

I smiled. I had this. Not sure how though, but I'd figure that out as I went along.

I leaped up at the big bot, then spun and hit him with a fart, right in the face. The bot stopped for a second. "How rude!" it told me. "My air sensors tell me that I am lucky I don't need to breathe air…"

Yes, I figured that fart wouldn't stop it, but it gave me time to think. I thought of eating ice cream in an igloo. Inhaling, I blasted the top of the bot with super cold breath.

The robot froze solid. I dropped to the ground.

The robot started to glow red. "Nice try, but I will just turn my internal heat controls up to melt this ice."

Now I had my chance. I leaped behind the robot. I grabbed one of its arms then leaped into the air and started spinning. The higher I went, the faster I spun. After ten or more rotations, I had created quite a lot of force. And the bot and I were way off the ground.

"Crashing from this height, won't harm me that much at all!" the robot laughed.

"I figured as much!"

Keeping my head straight as we spun, I saw the ground then space, the ground then space, the ground then space. I needed to time this just right. After about ten more rotations facing ground then space, I had the timing sorted out. I faced the ground. I rotated towards the sky. I forced myself to stop. I released my hold on the big bot, flinging it forward with all my might and sending it flying even higher into the sky. I hovered there. (Not sure how...) I watched as the robot soared higher and higher. With super vision, I saw the robot heating up. It kept flying higher and higher. I heard a little boom when the robot broke the sound barrier. I saw it drift off into space. Yep, it'd be no problem now!

I let myself glide back down to the ground.

"Yahoo! You tossed the robot out of the Earth's atmosphere! Yes, that cost my company millions of dollars, but money well spent!" I heard Dad say in my head.

I landed softly on the ground. "That was amazing!" Oscar Oranga said, rushing up to me. He stuck a microphone in my face. "Super Teen, any words for our viewers!"

I smiled and shrugged. "I just want to do my best!" I said.

Mom rushed over to me, holding her doctor's bag. "Super Teen, I'm a doctor, do you need any assistance?" she asked in her most official voice. She started looking me over from head to toe.

"I'm fine, doctor," I replied, in my most official voice.

Mom looked at my midsection, stopping at a large bullet hole in my shirt. She knelt down and examined the hole and looked for a wound.

"Oh my," she said in my head, which was even weirder with her being next to me. *"You must have been hit by a ricocheting bullet....but there's not even a burn mark on your skin..."*

I shrugged. *"Didn't feel it...."*

"Wow," Mom said out loud. "You are fine!"

I leaped up in the air and headed back towards my home. Yeah, I know my book bag and stuff were at school but after a day that featured an oral exam and a giant robot that I had to throw off Earth to defeat, I needed to get home.

That night after a long shower, I had a celebration pizza dinner with Mom, Grandma, Great Grandma, Jason, and strangely enough, Jessie and Tomas and Felipe. It turns out that Felipe being half-vampire really did know I was Super Teen all along. Man, that kid is sharp. So we had pretty much everybody who knew I was Super Teen at our house, except for my dad. Mom wouldn't let him in the door. I guess I couldn't blame her.

"To Lia!" Grandma Betsy said, raising a glass of milk to me!

"To Lia!" everybody else at the table joined in.

"Thanks, everyone! I couldn't have done it without you!" I grinned happily back at them.

We talked and ate into the night.

Dear Diary: OMG! What can I say or write? Unbelievable! I can hover in the air now to the point that it's like I'm flying. I am so strong I can throw a huge robot into outer space, at least when I'm angry. I feel I'm actually getting good at using my powers. I am developing some control. Plus, best of all, I gave an oral report and didn't do anything to embarrass myself. In fact, the report went really well. That actually felt as good as being super.

On the weird side (with me there's always a weird side), it's nice to have my father back in my life. Of course, it would be nicer if he didn't work for the company that created robots just to test me.

But, oh well, I guess no parent is perfect. ☺

Epilogue...

I laid awake in bed, checking my social media. Sure enough, some people complained about the damage Super Teen caused. I figured out that no matter what, you're never going to make everybody happy. On the bright side, many more people were happy that I saved the day and were impressed by what I did. Even Chief Michaels and Wendi commented on how that robot would have done major damage to the town if it weren't for Super Teen. Of course, Wendy did bring up the point that maybe BM Science would leave us alone if Super Teen wasn't around. More people blamed BM Science. BM Science joined the conversation, saying they were building the city a new park and recreation center.

My head hit the pillow knowing I had done well.

"Honey, are you awake?" I heard Dad in my mind.

I replied, *"Yes, Dad, I am!"*

"Sorry we had to do that to you, honey...."

"Yeah, it's kind of strange knowing my father helped design a gigantic robot to test my limits!" I mentally sighed.

"Believe me, honey, it's for the world's good!" Dad said in my head. (Yeah I'm still not used to that.)

"Ah, why?"

"Honey, aliens are coming! Earth will need you to be as strong as possible!"

The end for now...

Find out what happens next in
Diary of a Super Girl - Book 3.

Available NOW!

Thank you for reading Diary of a Super Girl: Book 2.
If you could leave a review, that would greatly help us to continue
to write more books.
Thank you so much!!!!!
Katrina and John

Here's some more books you may like:

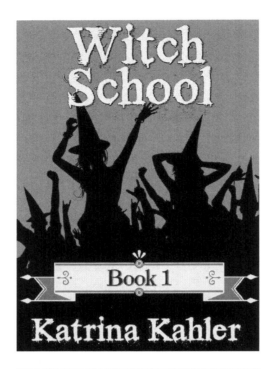

About the Authors

John Zakour *is a Humor/SF/Fantasy writer with a Master's Degree in Human Behavior. He has written thousands of gags for syndicated comics, comedians and TV Shows (including the Simpsons, Rugrats and Joan River's old TV show). John also writes a daily comic called Working Daze.*

Katrina Kahler *is the Best Selling Author of several series of books, including Julia Jones' Diary, Mind Reader, The Secret, Diary of a Horse Mad Girl, Twins, Angel, Slave to a Vampire and numerous Learn to Read Books for young children.*
Katrina lives in beautiful Noosa on the Australian coastline.

Printed in Great Britain
by Amazon